"Maybe You Need Protection."

"Out here?" Jessica laughed. "What in the world would I need protection from?"

The laughter was still on her lips as Dylan grabbed her and covered her mouth with his. He heard, as well as felt, her sharp intake of air.

She tasted like no other woman before. Intoxicating. Exciting. The passion shimmered between them as he ground his mouth against hers. Her lips parted, and he explored the sweetness of her with his tongue.

Jessica clung to Dylan, shocked by her own brazen response to his kiss. Her heart raced as his large hands cupped her bottom and pulled her fully against him. She moaned softly, needing to be closer still.

He released her suddenly, and she stumbled back. "That's what you need protection from," he said darkly. "Men like me."

Dear Reader,

As a very special treat this season, Silhouette Desire is bringing you the best in holiday stories. It's our gift from us—the editorial staff at Silhouette—to you, the readers. The month begins with a very special MAN OF THE MONTH from Ann Major, *A Cowboy Christmas*. Years ago, a boy and girl were both born under the same Christmas star. She grew up rich; he grew up poor…and when they met, they fell into a love that would last a lifetime….

Next, Anne McAllister's CODE OF THE WEST series continues with *Cowboys Don't Stay*, the third book in her series about the Tanner brothers.

Christmas weddings are always a lot of fun, and that's why we're bringing you *Christmas Wedding* by Pamela Macaluso. And if Texas is a place you'd like to spend the holidays—along with a sexy Texas man—don't miss *Texas Pride* by Barbara McCauley. Next, popular Silhouette Romance writer Sandra Steffen makes her Desire debut with *Gift Wrapped Dad*.

Finally, do not miss *Miracles and Mistletoe*, another compelling love story from the talented pen of Cait London.

So, from our "house" to yours…Happy Holidays.

Lucia Macro

Please address questions and book requests to:
Silhouette Reader Service
U.S.: 3010 Walden Ave., P.O. Box 1325, Buffalo, NY 14269
Canadian: P.O. Box 609, Fort Erie, Ont. L2A 5X3

BARBARA
McCAULEY
TEXAS PRIDE

SILHOUETTE *Desire*®
Published by Silhouette Books
America's Publisher of Contemporary Romance

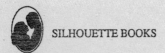

SILHOUETTE BOOKS

ISBN 0-373-05971-X

TEXAS PRIDE

Copyright © 1995 by Barbara Joel

Printed in U.S.A.

Books by Barbara McCauley

Silhouette Desire

Woman Tamer #621
Man from Cougar Pass #698
Her Kind of Man #771
Whitehorn's Woman #803
A Man Like Cade #832
Nightfire #875
*Texas Heat #917
*Texas Temptation #948
*Texas Pride #971

*Hearts of Stone

BARBARA McCAULEY

was born and raised in California and has spent a good portion of her life exploring the mountains, beaches and deserts so abundant there. The youngest of five children, she grew up in a small house, and her only chance for a moment alone was to sneak into the backyard with a book and quietly hide away.

With two children of her own now and a busy household, she still finds herself slipping away to enjoy a good novel. A daydreamer and incurable romantic, she says writing has fulfilled her most incredible dream of all—breathing life into the people in her mind and making them real. She has two loud and demanding Amazon parrots named Fred and Barney, and when she can manage the time, she loves to sink her hands into fresh-turned soil and make things grow.

This book is dedicated to all my readers.
Thank you for bringing the Stone family into your
hearts and homes.

And to Cristine Niessner, a special and talented editor
who believes in me and my ghosts.

One

"He's coming, Lucas! He just passed the farthest windmill, and he's headed right this way. It's him. I know it is!"

Lucas moved silently behind Margaret, intending to follow the direction of her gaze, but found himself watching her, instead. It was rare to see her so excited, and her pleasure brought him an unexpected warmth. Her pale blond hair shone silver and her slender transparent form had a luminescent aura. It had been a long time since he'd seen her glow this brightly. A very long time.

"It might not be him, Meggie," Lucas said gently, not wanting her to get her hopes too high. There had been too much unhappiness for her, and he couldn't bear to see her suffer even one more disappointment.

She turned to him, her green eyes wide, her lips curved into a smile. "No, Lucas. He's the one. I feel it."

Lucas knew better than to refute one of Meggie's "feelings." She'd been right too many times to ignore. Still, he wasn't sure he liked the idea of this man coming to Makeshift. He had become quite fond of Jessica Stone over the years, and he felt extremely protective of her.

"What a strange automobile he's driving," Meggie said, staring out the window again. "We've seen some unusual mechanical wagons over the years, but nothing quite like that. Do you think he lost some parts?"

The air vibrated with the sound of the vehicle, but Lucas still couldn't bring himself to look away from Meggie. She wore his favorite dress, the blue one that was as prim and proper as the schoolteacher herself. She'd had it on the first day they'd met. When she'd burst into his saloon, he'd thought she was going to scold him for teaching blackjack to her older students. Instead, she'd thanked him for instructing and encouraging her most difficult pupils in the use of mathematics.

An intense longing filled him, and though he knew it was impossible, the desire to touch her rose in him. He carefully traced the outline of her shoulders with his fingertips, remembering how soft and warm her skin had once felt.

Sensing rather than feeling his touch, Meggie turned and smiled sadly at Lucas. "We'll be together again," she said quietly. "I don't know how, my love, but I know we will."

She lifted a hand and spread her fingers. Lucas brought his palm to hers, dwarfing her small hand with his large one, carefully lining up his fingers with hers. The glow between them brightened and they both smiled.

Jessica Stone heard the deep rumble of a distant motorcycle and glanced up from the carton of books she'd been unpacking. With a frown, she wiped her hands on her jeans, then rose and went to the window of the second-story hotel room she'd moved into three days before. Hannibal, the German shepherd she'd rescued from the shelter in Cactus Flat, jumped up from his favorite spot—wherever Jessica was—and followed closely at her heels.

Eyes narrowed, Jessica stared at the approaching cloud of dust. The unusually hot weather West Texas was currently having so late in November created waves of shimmering heat off the barren plain. A dark figure emerged from those waves, and the sunlight glinted silver off the motorcycle's handlebars.

"I'm not expecting anyone," Jessica said to Hannibal. "How 'bout you?"

Hannibal tilted his large black head at his mistress, then barked once.

"I didn't think so." Jessica watched the bike slow as it neared the edge of Makeshift.

Normally Jessica liked being alone in the abandoned town she'd inherited when her father had died, but as she watched the lone rider park his motorcycle in front of the saloon across the street, she suddenly wished that Jake and Jared had stopped in today for one of their all-too-frequent, and all-too-obvious, visits.

Her brothers' overprotective behavior was a constant source of irritation. She knew, of course, that they only hovered over her because they loved her, but at twenty-seven, she thought herself capable of making her own decisions. Even if one of those decisions was to move out to Makeshift by herself.

Still, as she watched the biker pull off his helmet and give his long dark hair a shake, she wouldn't have minded a little company.

The man swung one long leg over his bike and stood with his back to her, both hands resting on his lean hips, and glanced around. He wore faded blue jeans and a black T-shirt, which stretched tightly over his wide back and muscular shoulders and arms. He was tall, at least as tall as Jake and Jared, who were both six foot four.

He turned and looked up directly at her.

Jessica sucked in a sharp breath and jumped away from the window. Hannibal barked at her sudden movement.

"Shush!" She put a finger to her lips. The dog wagged his tail and pressed his nose against her knee.

She waited a few moments, letting her heart calm before she peeked out the window again.

He was gone.

She moved closer to the window and glanced from one end of the town to the other, but she saw nothing. A dust devil picked up a tumbleweed in front of the general store and kicked it down the wooden sidewalk.

"Where did he go?" she muttered, frowning at the empty streets. The town wasn't that big, and except for the saloon and the hotel, most of the buildings were still boarded up.

A low growl rumbled from Hannibal. The dog jumped away from Jessica and turned, his ears laid back and his teeth bared.

Jessica froze, and she knew without a doubt that the stranger was standing in the doorway behind her.

She turned slowly and stared into eyes the darkest brown she'd ever seen. For a moment, she could have sworn he appeared as surprised as she was, but the look was quickly gone, and a disinterested nonchalance was all that remained. He leaned against the doorjamb, his arms folded. His gaze shifted from her to Hannibal.

"Nice dog."

The stranger's voice was deep and rough, and Hannibal responded to the sound with a short bark. Jessica laid a hand on the dog's head, whether to calm the animal or herself she wasn't sure.

"Can I help you with something?" she asked, wishing that the man wasn't blocking the only easy exit from the room. His tall frame practically filled the doorway. Close up, she could see the muscles she'd only guessed at from across the street. There was a rugged strength that emanated from him, a masculinity that frightened her, yet at the same time also pricked at the most basic, primitive female instinct. He was pure sensuality, and her breath caught as she stared at him.

He pushed away from the doorjamb, and the movement caused Hannibal to growl again. "You Jessica Stone?"

It should have comforted her that he knew her name. It didn't. "Yes."

"I heard you're looking for a foreman."

Jessica frowned. She'd filled out the paperwork, but the advertisement wasn't scheduled to be in the paper until the next day. "And how did you hear that?"

"In town. Couple of guys at the diner were talking."

That was certainly possible. If there was one thing people did in a small town, it was talk. There'd been quite a buzz in Cactus Flat that Jessica Stone had received a grant to convert Makeshift into a center for troubled youth. Most of the townspeople supported her, but there were a few who were adamantly opposed to the idea. Her stepmother, Myrna, was at the head of that list. Not because she was so against helping teenagers, but because the annoying woman wanted the land for herself.

"I haven't interviewed anyone yet," she said. "The ad comes out tomorrow."

"Cancel it and hire me."

He said the words with such confidence Jessica almost agreed. That would go over well with Jared and Jake. They'd certainly understand she hired this biker guy because he told her to. "I hardly think I should hire the first man who shows up."

"No," he agreed. "You should hire the best man."

She lifted one eyebrow. "And that's you?"

He grinned. Jessica felt her insides twist and turn at the flash of straight white teeth. "You have a name?" she asked.

"Dylan Grant."

"And your qualifications, Mr. Grant?"

"Sixteen years in the business. You name it, I've done it."

She certainly believed that. Something told Jessica there was much more to that statement than the obvious. There was a hard edge in his eyes and in the way he held himself that spoke volumes about his life experience, though she guessed him to be only in his early thirties. And he certainly appeared capable. It was clear he was a man who made his living with physical work. His T-shirt defined the iron muscles in his upper arms and shoulders, his skin was tan and his big hands looked rough and callused.

Jessica suddenly realized she was staring. She pulled her gaze back to his and saw the amusement in his dark eyes. She cursed the blush slowly working its way over her cheeks.

"What brings you out this way?" she asked, forcing a businesslike tone into her voice. "Cactus Flat is hardly a tourist hot spot."

Dylan winced. "I've been called a lot of things," he drawled, "but never a tourist. That's cutting pretty deep."

Dammit. There was that smile again. Jessica bit the inside of her lip and ignored the flutter in her stomach. "This project is very important to me, Mr. Grant. It's a relatively small job, a reconstruction of a few of the buildings here. It's not long-term, but I need a responsible, dependable man to run a crew. Drifters and restless bikers are hardly what I consider reliable."

"No matter what I am, Miss Stone," he said flatly, "I keep my word. If nothing else, you can count on that."

She hadn't meant to offend him, but when it came to rebuilding Makeshift, Jessica could take no chances.

"I'm acting as my own general contractor," she said. "Do you have any problem working for a woman?"

"Can't say. I've never worked for a woman before."

She couldn't help but smile. "At least you're honest, Mr. Grant. That's nearly as important as experience."

Dylan's eyes narrowed. Her heart skipped when he moved into the room toward her. Hannibal gave another short growl when the stranger knelt and held out his hand.

"If there's one thing I have, Miss Stone," Dylan said, reaching his fingers toward Hannibal, "it's experience."

Dylan gave an inward sigh of relief that his hand was still intact as he pet the dog. There was no doubt that if he'd attempted a move toward Jessica the animal would have gone for his throat. *Good dog,* he thought, and scratched behind the animal's ear.

Hannibal wagged his tail.

The animal's mistress was a little more apprehensive, Dylan noted, allowing himself a slow upward perusal of Jessica's long denim-clad legs and curved hips. She'd rolled the sleeves of her white cotton blouse to her elbows, revealing slender smooth-skinned arms, and it was impossible not to notice the press of her rounded breasts against the thin cloth.

He forced his gaze upward still, and she tucked a long strand of dark shiny hair behind her ear, watching him warily with eyes that were a deep rich blue. He'd seen that color before, once, in another place and another time. But there was something about these particular eyes that made his gut tighten and his pulse quicken.

He didn't like the feeling one bit.

He wrenched his gaze away and stood. "What exactly is it you're doing out here, Miss Stone? It's a little off the beaten track for a shopping mall."

She bristled at his statement. "Shopping has never been a hobby of mine. I'm converting Makeshift into a camp for teenagers."

"Makeshift?"

She nodded. "My great-great-grandfather, Josiah Stone, founded this town in 1873 after he bought Stone Creek and started ranching. Cattlemen needed a place for supplies and rest when they were driving their herds to New Mexico. The first structure built was the saloon." She looked out the window and gestured across the street.

"Important things first," Dylan said with a grin.

"Exactly." She smiled back. "The town boomed for twenty-five years, until railroads took over. Mining kept it going a few more years, but that dwindled, too. A few die-hards stayed on and took care of the place, but they've been gone since the forties. When my father, J. T. Stone, died earlier this year, we found out he'd divided Stone Creek into four parcels, one for each of my brothers and half sister, and one—Makeshift—for me."

Dylan looked around the small hotel room. A patchwork quilt covered a large brass bed, and two antique oak night-stands held matching stained-glass oil lamps. Several framed paintings covered the freshly painted walls, and a large cherry armoire stood open, revealing several gowns of an era long past.

Dylan shook his head in amazement. The room had ob-viously been restored to its original condition with care. The only thing out of place here was the telephone sitting on the floor beside three cardboard boxes of books and a radio on a nightstand. Otherwise, he might have thought he'd stepped over some invisible time line and been transported into the previous century.

He gestured at the bed. "Are you living out here by yourself?"

She glanced away, but not before he saw the flicker of uncertainty in her eyes. "I'm not alone. I have Hannibal, and one of my two brothers is usually close by. They aren't crazy about my living out here, so they stop by often."

He stood close enough to catch the light scent of jasmine that drifted from her skin. He resisted the urge to lean even closer and pull the fragrance more deeply into his lungs. "I don't see anyone here now."

She brought her gaze back to his with an intensity that surprised him. "What you see—or don't see—can be very deceiving, Mr. Grant."

As she continued to stare at him, Dylan felt as if a weight were pressing on his chest. The air in the room seemed to grow heavy and he found it difficult to breathe. Hannibal stood suddenly, his ears pricked, and started to bark.

The sensation eased, then disappeared. The Texas heat was definitely getting to him, Dylan thought as he drew in a deep breath and stepped to the armoire. "Interesting wardrobe."

Jessica moved beside him. "They were my great-great-grandmother's. My mother kept them and everything else here in storage. I still have more furniture, plus several large trunks in my brother's attic that I haven't had time to bring here and go through."

A smile curved Jessica's lips as she reached out and touched one black silk evening gown. Dylan felt a jolt of electricity move up and down his arm as she stroked the lace sleeve of the dress with her long slender fingers.

Jessica Stone was certainly a surprise. And he didn't like surprises. He realized that if he was going to be working with this woman, he was going to have to keep his distance.

The hardwood floor creaked beneath his boots as he stepped away from her and glanced around the room. "Is this the only room you've restored?"

She shook her head. "The bedroom next door, also, and the connecting bathroom has modern conveniences, plus there's electricity in the kitchen for the refrigerator. But the only thing I get credit for is the paint. My brothers fought my moving out here every step of the way, but once they knew I couldn't be swayed, they reluctantly gave in and took over. At least I have indoor plumbing and electricity now."

Dylan moved to the window and stared down at the empty street. The buildings themselves, though worn and faded with the years, appeared structurally sound. "Exactly what kind of camp are you intending to build here?"

"Maybe youth center is a better description," Jessica said as she closed the armoire doors. "A place for kids to get away from the problems of modern-day life."

Frowning, he turned to look at her. "You mean you want to turn this place into a playground for juvenile delinquents?"

Jessica realized that not everyone could understand what she was trying to do here, but she still couldn't help the irritation that shot through her at this man's ignorance. She could explain to him how Makeshift had turned her own life around, but she doubted he would understand. It was also none of his business.

"Teenagers need all the help they can get these days. I want to give them a place they can come to if things get rough. Let them know that someone cares. If you have a problem with that concept, I suggest you apply for another job."

He shrugged. "You can build a bridge here if it makes you happy. One job is like any other to me. It would just seem more practical to sell this land and build something closer to town."

"This is Stone Creek, Mr. Grant. I wouldn't consider selling even one acre of what my father has left me, practical or not. Once the review board approves my construction progress in early January, I'll have my license, and Makeshift will be a legitimate state-approved youth center."

"And if they don't approve the progress?" he asked.

"They have to approve it," she said firmly. Her chest tightened at the very thought that they might not. As if sensing her tension, Hannibal slipped his head under Jessica's hand.

Dylan folded his arms and leaned against the windowsill. "So when do we start?"

We? Jessica bit back the first answer that came to mind and went with the second, more polite one. "I'm interviewing for the position tomorrow in town. One o'clock at the Bronco Diner in Cactus Flat." She moved to a nightstand

and opened the top drawer. "Fill out this application and we'll talk then."

His gaze held hers, and even though he took the form from her, he never once glanced at it. "Shall I get there early to avoid the rush?"

"I'm sure that won't be necessary," she said dryly, annoyed that he was making fun of her. "Just take a number and be seated."

He held out his hand. "Until tomorrow, then, Miss Stone."

Jessica hesitated, then placed her fingers in his palm. The texture of his skin was rough, and she felt a shiver run up her arm. His scent was masculine, the warmth of his touch disarming.

Quickly she pulled her hand away. "Tomorrow, Mr. Grant."

He pushed away from the windowsill, then bent and rubbed Hannibal's head. The animal seemed to smile at him. "See ya later, pal."

Jessica struggled to compose herself as Dylan crossed the room. When he turned abruptly at the doorway, her breath caught.

"I think your brothers are right, Jessica," he said. "You shouldn't be out here alone."

He turned and left then, whistling a Bob Seger tune. She moved to the window and watched as he walked to his motorcycle and pulled on his helmet. When he glanced up at her, she didn't even pretend not to be looking. He grinned, then got on his bike and left.

Jessica exhaled sharply. Her knees felt shaky as she sat on the edge of her bed. Hannibal laid his head on her lap.

"Some watchdog you are," she murmured, absently stroking the animal's soft fur. "If you could talk, you probably would've invited him to dinner."

Hannibal looked up at her and wagged his tail.

"I'm not hiring him," she said firmly, taking the dog's head in her hands and staring into his eyes. "I don't need any distractions right now, and that man is trouble with a capital *T*."

Hannibal whined, then barked softly.

"No." She shook her head. "I need to concentrate on Makeshift right now. Everyone in my youth group is counting on me. There are too many kids out there who desperately need a place like this. I haven't time for romantic notions, especially concerning arrogant men who obviously don't understand the importance of what I'm doing here. Mr. Dylan Grant is going to have to find another job somewhere else."

Jessica stood, nearly tripping over Hannibal as he circled her knees. She scooted him away, wondering what in the world had gotten into the dog. He'd never acted like this before.

She moved to the window, looking down at the street, and felt the steady beating of her heart. Come to think of it, *she'd* never acted this way before, either.

All the more reason not to hire the man, she told herself, then turned her attention back to the box of books she'd been unpacking. She lifted one heavy volume on the Old West and smiled. As of one o'clock tomorrow, Mr. Dylan Grant would be like the book in her hand—history.

"Oh, Lucas, isn't Mr. Grant wonderful?" Meggie asked as she watched the motorcycle disappear. "He's absolutely perfect for Jessica."

Lucas stood in front of the hotel beside Meggie, his arms firmly folded. "I knew a man named Grant once. From Cheyenne. Town hung him for horse stealing."

"The president of the United States also happens to be named Grant. Or at least he was president." Meggie put her hands on her hips and faced Lucas. "Anyway, you're just being overprotective."

Lucas frowned. "I am not."

"Oh, really? Then what was that little business in the hotel room when Mr. Grant got a little too close to Jessica? I suppose it was a coincidence he suddenly couldn't breathe? If Hannibal hadn't stopped you, you might have hurt the poor man."

"I didn't like what he was thinking."

Meggie lifted one brow. "And since when can you read minds? That ability is for Hannibal only. And if Hannibal likes Dylan Grant, which he does, then that's good enough for me."

With a flip of her head, Meggie turned and moved across the street to the saloon. Lucas watched her go, admiring the slender figure that had once been warm and firm under his touch. He smiled, remembering the soft moans she'd made when he'd kissed her the first time, and the shy touch of her hands on his body one afternoon in a small secluded cave not far from town.

His smile faded, and he stared out at the Texas plain. Something was happening. Lucas had felt it the instant Dylan walked into Jessica's room. It was something powerful, something important. He was filled with an overwhelming feeling of anticipation, a mixture of excitement and dread.

Lucas cursed his inability to understand what was taking place. Despite what people thought, ghosts had limitations and restrictions. He knew that something was going to happen, but he had no idea what it was. He also had no idea if it would be good, or if it would be bad.

He only knew that the minute Dylan Grant had come into town, none of them—Jessica, Dylan, Meggie and himself—would ever be the same.

Two

___

Dylan sat in the corner booth of the Bronco Diner, his legs stretched out comfortably under the table, and sipped a cup of hot coffee a pretty little brunette waitress kept filled. He'd polished off a hamburger and french fries a few minutes ago, then settled back with his coffee to enjoy the entertainment, which was watching Jessica in another booth across the aisle interview an interesting assortment of potential foremen.

She'd dressed very businesslike today, Dylan noted. Her navy blue suit was tailored, the skirt resting conservatively at her knees. She'd buttoned her white blouse to the neck and tightly pulled her dark hair to the back of her head, held there by a gold barrette. It was an obvious but futile attempt to downplay her femininity and discourage male interest.

Didn't she realize that by dressing so severely she actually encouraged a man's fantasy? Dylan had seen the way the men had looked at her: like they wanted to strip that suit off, pull her hair loose, then drag her slim body underneath their own. The woman was too naive for her own good, Dylan thought, his irritation building as each man took the seat across from Jessica.

Her sixth and current applicant, a long-nosed, thin-haired redhead, had never actually worked in construction, he explained, but had helped his brother-in-law build a carport once. When the man proceeded to describe the building of the structure in excruciating detail, Jessica quickly thanked him for coming and told him she'd call as soon as she made her decision.

Dylan had given Jessica his application over an hour ago, but she had yet to call him. Every time she finished an interview, she'd smile at him, then call someone else. Since there was only one more applicant left, a heavyset man with whiskers, she couldn't put off the inevitable much longer.

And since he had all the time in the world, Dylan ordered a piece of apple pie and settled back to wait.

The interview ended quickly after the heavyset man referred to Jessica as "girlie."

When she finally turned to Dylan, he raised his brows and gave her a blank look. She frowned at him, then picked up one application and crossed over to him. She looked tired, he thought. And frustrated.

"Mr. Grant," she said, staring at the form in her hand, "I've gone over your application."

He gestured for her to sit across from him. "Is there a problem?"

She hesitated, then tugged off her jacket and sat.

"I'd say so. You have a structural-engineering degree from Indiana University, and you've worked on everything from high-rise construction to the building of bridges in the jungles of South America."

"Does that disqualify me?"

"No, it overqualifies you." She stretched her neck with a weary sigh, then undid the top button of her blouse. "Mr. Grant, did you read my ad in the paper this morning?"

He forced himself not to look as her fingers fiddled with the button. "My name is Dylan, and yes, I did read your ad."

"Then you know how much I can afford to pay?"

He nodded.

"And you still want the job?"

She unclipped the barrette from her hair. Dylan watched as she shook her head and pulled her fingers through the thick strands. He felt hotter than the weather warranted, and his pulse began to pound.

He had to remind himself she'd asked him a question, then searched his brain to remember what it was. "Yes. I do want the job."

She shook her head in disbelief. "I don't get it. You can have your pick of jobs and make ten times the salary anywhere else. Why in the world would you come here and work for the proverbial peanuts?"

"Would you like some more coffee, Dylan?"

Jessica glanced up at the waitress, Susan Davis, and frowned again. *Dylan?* Wasn't it strange, she thought irritably, that she'd been sitting in this restaurant for over an hour and she'd had her cup refilled only once? She was sure Dylan's cup had never dropped more than a quarter inch. So what if he filled out a T-shirt and jeans well? So what if that long dark hair and rough slow-talking voice made a woman's knees turn to water? She was a customer here, too, and the waitress's selective efficiency was quickly grating on Jessica's nerves. And so was the smile Dylan was so warmly displaying.

"Thanks, Susan." Dylan pushed his cup closer. "And bring the lady here a hamburger and fries, please. I think she worked up an appetite interviewing all those men."

Susan? It certainly hadn't taken him long to get chummy, Jessica thought. "Never mind. I'm not staying that long."

"I'll have seconds, then," Dylan said with a shrug. "Extra cheese."

Susan bounced off, happy to oblige.

Exasperated, Jessica leaned back against the vinyl cushions and kicked off her heels. She closed her eyes and breathed her contentment.

Dylan glanced under the table, then raised one brow. "Is taking off our clothes part of the interview?"

She frowned at him. "My shoes are too tight."

He grinned back. "Your skirt is tight, also," he said with a note of hope in his voice.

"My skirt stays on," she said coolly. "And I'm not interviewing you anymore."

"Does that mean I'm hired?"

She shook her head.

"So who are you going to hire?" he asked. "The fat guy who 'accidentally' bumped your knee six times and dropped his pencil under the table four times?"

Jessica felt a fresh wave of anger just thinking about that lecher. She'd had to refrain from kicking him the last time he'd dropped the damn pencil. "Of course not. But since you were paying such close attention, you must have noticed that Mr. Thompson, my second applicant, was highly qualified. He was a carpenter for a housing developer in San Antonio and an electrician for a small construction company in Austin."

"Oh, yes." Dylan took a swig of coffee. "Mr. Thompson. The guy whose hands were shaking."

"He was a little nervous, that's all."

"I'm sure that's why he left here and went straight to that bar across the street."

Jessica sighed with resignation and tucked her legs beneath her chair. "A pretty sorry lot."

"And at the salary you're offering, you won't get better," Dylan said pointedly.

"Except for you."

He grinned at her. "Of course."

And just who *was* he? she wondered. Other than the fact he was thirty-four and born in Maine, his application had been sketchy regarding his personal life. There'd been no mention of a wife—or wives, as the case might be—or children.

Damn that smile of his. She hated the way it made her control slip. He sipped his coffee, watching her with dark intense eyes that never seemed to miss a thing. She shifted slightly under his perusal.

"Which brings me back to my question," she said with a calm she didn't feel. "With your qualifications, why would you accept what I'm offering?"

Susan set the hamburger and fries in front of Dylan, fussed over him for a minute, then when Jessica scowled at her, reluctantly moved to take another order at the counter.

Dylan slid the plate closer to Jessica. The smell of the fries was sheer heaven. *Just one,* she told herself, reaching for the plate.

"The first reason is that it's temporary work, nothing long-term," he said. "I don't like to be tied down."

No big surprise there, Jessica thought. A man who traveled on a motorcycle with little more than a duffel bag was hardly the type to build picket fences. "And your second reason?" she asked.

"This youth center you want to build," Dylan said, "are you doing it for money?"

"Of course not," she answered impatiently.

"And the land, Stone Creek, you could sell it and make a few bucks?"

Even the thought of selling one acre of Stone Creek sent a wave of indignation through Jessica. "I told you I would never sell."

"So everything doesn't have to be about money, does it?" Dylan asked. "There are other reasons that motivate people, aren't there?"

Dylan saw the suspicion in Jessica's blue eyes. Not that he blamed her. He'd certainly be suspicious if he were in her place. He hadn't even listed all his past experience, but since he wasn't sure of the competition, he'd given her enough to assure him the job. He just had to convince her he was the right man.

The problem was he wasn't so sure anymore that he *was* the right man. He hadn't been prepared for his reaction to Jessica. Even as he watched her now, with her hair loose and the top of her blouse undone, he felt a wave of overwhelming lust for her. That was all it was, of course. Lust. But it was certainly stronger than anything he'd experienced before. And it certainly would complicate matters. As she nibbled delicately on a french fry, he couldn't stop the sweat breaking out on his skin.

He'd have to control his more basic instincts, that was all. Jessica was off-limits. Way off-limits.

"Okay, Mr. Grant," she said, finally breaking the long silence.

"Dylan."

She nodded. "Okay, Dylan. So maybe there are other reasons that motivate people. Tell me what yours are. I think you owe me at least that much."

He thought about that for a moment. "Let's just say I've never done anything like this before."

"Another notch in the experience belt, huh?"

"Something like that."

Jessica couldn't stop the corners of her mouth from curving upward. It was hard to believe, incredible even, that a man with Dylan's qualifications would work for the pay she offered. "Christmas is just a few weeks away. Are you going to need time off to be with your family?"

He shook his head. "There's no notch in my belt for family, Miss Stone. Christmas is just another day to me."

She couldn't imagine anyone feeling that way about Christmas. It was her favorite holiday. The most special day of the year, as far as she was concerned. She was torn between being happy he didn't need time off and feeling sorry for him. Dylan, however, did not appear to be a man that wanted sympathy from anyone.

"All right, then." She met his steady gaze. "You're hired."

"There is one more thing."

"What's that?"

"I need a room."

She nearly choked. "What!"

"Your salary isn't enough to live on. I need a place to stay."

What was the saying? If something was too good to be true, then it probably wasn't? "I can't afford that. It would cost a fortune to rent you a room here in town."

"I don't want to stay here. I want to stay out at Makeshift, to cut down on travel time and the expense of gas. Plus, if there's any problems, I'll be right there."

It didn't matter that everything he said made sense. It wasn't possible. "You can't be serious. I can't stay out there with you, alone."

"Why not?"

Her cheeks flushed bright red. "Because...well, because I can't."

"I won't attack you, Jessica, if that's what you're afraid of. All I'm interested in here is a job."

She was glad to hear that, but nevertheless, her ego still winced at the outright rejection. "I'm most certainly not afraid. It's just that, well, I like my privacy and..." She straightened the silverware on the table and fiddled with the napkin.

"And your brothers will kill you?"

She shook her head. "No. They'll kill you most likely."

"Let me worry about your brothers. I'm sure they're reasonable men."

"Reasonable?" Jessica gave a dry laugh. "Dylan, that word doesn't exist when describing the Stone men." She spread her hands wide and sighed. "But it certainly will be interesting to watch you try."

"So I'm hired?"

She couldn't believe she was doing this. She was insane. Although, she'd be equally insane *not* to do everything necessary to employ this man. She smiled at him and held out her hand. "You're hired."

Dylan smiled back and took her hand. The connection was like grabbing a live wire. They stared at each other, each of them stunned at the awareness that radiated between them.

Dylan quickly let go, relieved that the waitress had chosen exactly that moment to refill his coffee cup and chatter about how much she liked motorcycles. He nodded politely, though he barely heard more than a few words, and wondered what the hell he'd gotten himself into.

"You did *what?*"

Jessica stood in the mesquite-clogged street in front of Makeshift Saloon and silently tolerated Jared's yelling. Arms folded, Jake stood beside his brother, his face set in hard lines beneath his black Stetson.

"I told you," she explained patiently, combing her hair back from her face when a warm breeze caught the loose ends, "yesterday I hired a man named Dylan Grant to be my foreman, and part of his salary is a room here. I expect him any minute now, and I want you both to behave yourselves."

"How could you do something so idiotic?" Jared continued. "You don't even know this guy. How do you know he's not a serial killer?"

"Because I know." Jessica put her hands on her hips and looked at her brothers. They both had the same black hair and Stone-blue eyes as she did. Anyone else having a confrontation with two six-foot-four-inch angry men might be intimidated, but Jessica had learned at a very young age to stand her ground. "And Hannibal liked him, too." She scratched the dog behind his ears.

Jake rolled his eyes, and Jared threw his hands up.

"Oh, I feel much better now," Jared said, taking a step toward the dog. When Hannibal growled, Jared frowned and moved back.

Jessica smiled. "See. I told you he's a good judge of character. I'm still trying to figure out what Annie sees in you, sweet-tempered man that you are. By the way, how are the wedding plans going? It's only two weeks away."

"Everything is going fine," Jared replied. "And don't try and change the subject."

"We'll talk about Jared's wedding later," Jake said flatly, tipping back his hat. "Right now you've got some explaining to do."

Jessica sighed and faced her oldest brother. It had always been a little easier to get around Jared than Jake. Since their father had died, Jake had taken his position as head of the family very seriously. A little too seriously at the moment, she thought with annoyance.

Time to change tactics, she decided.

"Jared, Jake—" she moved between her brothers and looked up at them "—you know I love you both, and I wouldn't do anything to upset you. Just meet Dylan, talk to him. I'm sure you'll feel the same way I do about him."

Well, maybe not *quite* the same way, Jessica amended silently. Her body was still humming from that simple handshake yesterday. She'd tried to tell herself she'd just been so relieved to find a foreman after all those terrible interviews that she'd overreacted to his touch.

But if nothing else, she was honest. And the truth was she was attracted to the man. In a big way.

It doesn't matter. She had no intention of encouraging any attention from Dylan Grant. She'd made the mistake once of getting involved with someone she'd worked with, and the results had been less than wonderful.

Besides, Dylan had made it clear he wanted work, nothing else. *Temporary* work. She had the feeling "temporary" was the man's middle name.

The ground started to shake and the air vibrate. Jake and Jared looked up sharply, their eyes narrowed as they turned in the direction of the sound. Hannibal's ears lifted.

"He rides a *motorcycle?*" Jared said.

"Similar to the one you used to ride six or seven years ago," Jessica reminded Jared.

She held her breath as Dylan roared up, leaving a billowing trail of dust in his wake. He parked the bike in front of the saloon and stepped off, pulling the helmet from his head.

The three men faced each other like gunfighters from the Old West. All they needed, Jessica decided, were gun belts slung low on their hips and spurs on their boots.

This is ridiculous, she thought, and turned toward Dylan with a smile, even though her insides were quaking. Hannibal barked and bounded over to Dylan with an enthusiastic wag of his tail.

Jessica threw her brothers an "I told you so" look. They frowned back.

Dylan knelt and greeted the dog, then straightened and moved toward Jessica. "Mornin'." He nodded at the two other men.

"Dylan Grant, these are my brothers, Jake—" Dylan met and held Jake's dark gaze as they shook hands "—and Jared."

Jared all but scowled at Dylan as he took his hand. Jessica could have sworn there was amusement in Dylan's eyes

as the handshake progressed into a test of strength. She was
ready to step between the two when Jared suddenly let go.

She realized she'd been holding her breath and slowly let
it out.

That was when the barrage of questioning began. Jessica
knew she couldn't stop it, so she simply stood back and
waited. She already knew most of Dylan's background as
far as construction went, but nothing of his personal life.
When Jake moved into that territory, Jessica found herself
listening closely.

"You have a wife or a family?" Jake asked.

Dylan's eyes narrowed. "Does it matter?"

"If something happens to you it will," Jake said evenly.
"We'll need to know who to notify."

Jessica wanted to kick Jake. Although his question was
certainly a logical one, there was an undertone of a threat in
it, as well. And based on the dark expression on Dylan's
face, he hadn't missed the warning.

"I'm not married," Dylan said flatly. "Something happens to me—" he held Jake's steady gaze "—you'll have to
deal with it."

"Well, then," Jake said with a nod, "I guess we'll just
have to watch real close and make sure nothing happens to
you."

The "watch real close" part rankled Jessica, but at least
the tension eased somewhat. Jessica's breathing had almost
returned to normal by the time Jake shook Dylan's hand
again.

"My wife, Savannah, is having a dinner party for Jared
and his fiancée, Annie, tomorrow night at the ranch," Jake
said to Dylan. "Sort of a prewedding celebration. Why
don't you come along with Jessica?"

Jessica had to close her mouth as she stared at Jake. She
couldn't have heard what she'd thought she just heard. *Jake*
inviting *Dylan* to dinner? Not possible. Even Jared seemed
to accept the idea without complaint, though he still

watched Dylan warily. No doubt they wanted to interrogate the man further.

"Much obliged." Dylan nodded at Jake. "I'll be there."

Jessica couldn't find her voice to utter a word when Jake and Jared kissed her goodbye. Their boots crunched on the gravel as they walked to Jake's pickup and got in. They drove off, leaving a cloud of dust billowing behind them.

She'd been surprised when they'd finally quit harassing her about moving out here, but this, *this,* was unbelievable. They'd not only invited Dylan for dinner, they were actually giving in and letting him stay in Makeshift. With her. Alone.

The realization suddenly made her palms sweat.

She turned to Dylan, equally amazed that he'd handled the cross-examination as well as he had, even when the questions had turned personal.

"I'm sorry about that," she said.

"That they invited me for dinner?"

"No, of course not. About the grilling they just gave you."

"They care about you, Jessica," Dylan said quietly, squinting into the late-morning sun as he watched the pickup disappear. "That's nothing to be sorry about."

There was something in Dylan's voice, a wistfulness or perhaps a regret, that brought an unexplained ache to Jessica's chest.

"I know what it's like to lose your parents," she said softly. "I'm sorry."

He looked at her with surprise. "Thank you, but my parents are alive and well somewhere in Europe right now, I imagine. Not together, of course," he added. "Most likely with the current spouse or live-in friend."

Confused, she stared at him. "But you said you had no family."

"I said I had no wife. As far as my family goes, we rarely see each other. Like I told your brother, if there's a problem here, you'll have to handle it."

Jessica had always been so close to her parents it was difficult to understand that kind of indifference. But Dylan's personal life was none of her business, she told herself, and from the curt tone of his voice, she knew he wasn't offering any more information.

Quiet seemed to surround them. The breeze picked up and gently swung the wooden sign over what used to be the doctor's office. The swinging doors of the saloon creaked. She suddenly had no idea what to do with her hands. She clasped them in front of her and turned awkwardly to Dylan. "So, uh, where do we start?"

Dylan stared at Jessica and tried not to notice how snug her jeans were or how the T-shirt she wore defined the roundness of her breasts. He could think of a few places he'd like to start with this woman, most of them involving a bed and fewer clothes. He sighed inwardly. That line of thinking was only going to lead to trouble, so he forced it from his mind.

"How about a tour?" he suggested. "I need to take a closer look at the insides of the buildings and see what kind of condition they're in. After I look at your blueprints, I can make a materials list."

"Well," she said tentatively, glancing quickly away, then back again, "there is a slight problem there."

"A slight problem where?" he asked, though something told Dylan he wasn't going to like the answer.

"Well, I don't exactly have any blueprints."

He was right. He didn't like the answer. "You didn't call in an architect on a project this size?"

"Oh, I called one, all right. I just couldn't afford him. All I have are a few preliminary sketches and permits for the work Jake and Jared did. I thought maybe I could just sort of figure it out as I went along."

Dylan stared at Jessica in disbelief. "Let me get this straight. You thought you could just figure out how to rebuild this entire town—without blueprints?"

"Actually," Jessica said, her expression full of guilt, "I was hoping you . . . well, whoever I hired, I mean, might be able to handle it."

He struggled not to raise his voice. "Me? On the salary you're paying me, I'm supposed to spend God knows how many hours drawing up plans, too?"

"I don't expect anything, Dylan," she said, holding his gaze with her own. "If you don't want to do it, I'm sure I can manage to pull something together for you."

"You don't *pull* together blueprints, Jessica," he said sharply. "You *draw* them. Slowly and carefully."

This job of his was getting increasingly more complicated by the moment, Dylan thought with annoyance. Hell, before long, this woman would probably have *him* paying *her* for the privilege of working here. If he had an ounce of sense or a lick of pride, he'd get back on his bike and keep riding.

But this job had nothing to do with sense or pride, he reminded himself. With a sigh, he ran his hands through his hair and faced Jessica.

And the instant he looked at her, he knew he'd never ride on out. Her eyes, a soft deep blue, were wide as she stared back at him. A man could drown in those eyes. There was passion there. Determination. The combination of the two was deadly. He'd never met anyone like her before. Two days ago he'd have laughed at the idea that anyone like her even existed.

But here she was, standing in front of him, her chin tilted upward, her eyes bright. She was a dreamer. An idealist. She hadn't learned yet that people couldn't be trusted. That they were only out to get what they wanted for themselves.

She'd learn soon enough.

He stepped closer to her. "All right. I'll do it. But with all this extra work and no pay, I'm going to need a little incentive." He lowered his voice as he searched her face. "Something to make it worth my while."

Her body stiffened at his suggestive tone, and when her gaze locked with his, anger darkened her eyes. "And what exactly would you consider worth your while, Mr. Grant?"

He leaned closer still, bringing his face within inches of hers. "You have to cook for me."

Dylan struggled not to laugh when Jessica's lips parted in surprise, and when he found himself staring at that enticing mouth longer than good sense dictated, he straightened and backed away.

"You want me to cook for you?"

He nodded. "You do know how to cook, don't you?"

"Of course I know how to cook." She frowned. "But there's no usable kitchen in Makeshift. Unless I go to town or to one of my brothers' places, it's sandwiches and raw vegetables."

"Sandwiches are fine for lunch, but I want a hot meal at night and a big breakfast every morning." He took malicious delight in the gasp Jessica uttered. "And if I see so much as one raw vegetable, I'm out of here."

She folded her arms and faced him. "And just how do you expect me to cook without a stove or oven?"

"Well—" Dylan scratched at his chin thoughtfully "—people ate hot food here before, didn't they?"

"Yes," she answered carefully.

"So I guess if you were going to figure out how to rebuild this town without blueprints, you can figure out how to cook without electricity."

Cook without electricity? Jessica stared at him. She was still reeling from his first assault on her senses, when she'd thought he was about to proposition her. She'd been furious, of course, and ready to tell him where he could go. And yet, at the same time, she'd felt an excitement course through her. Then when he'd told her he wanted her to cook for him, he'd caught her completely off guard again. She'd always been so sure of herself. Of who she was and what she wanted. For the first time, she felt off-key and out of balance.

She didn't like it one bit.

This project, like the man standing in front of her, was getting more complicated by the minute. But what choice did she have? She had no idea where to begin, but as he'd said, she'd figure it out.

She sighed heavily and shook her head. "All right, Dylan. But let's hope it won't be your words you eat, instead of my food. Either one is going to be hard to chew."

"He's staying, Lucas! He's staying!"

Lucas smiled as Meggie floated upward toward the saloon ceiling and spun. He'd never tire of watching her. One hundred and twenty years hadn't dimmed that pleasure.

"I will reserve my judgment on that just now," Lucas said. "I most certainly didn't like his provocative manner of speaking to her."

"Oh, yes, he is a rogue, isn't he?" She smiled brightly. "But I knew he was teasing her. And you did, too, or you would have stopped him."

Lucas nodded. "I admit I admire his resourcefulness. But I'm not sure why Jessica would object to cooking for him."

Meggie floated back down and faced Lucas. "I suppose you think a woman should be thrilled at the idea of slaving over a hot stove for a man all day?"

Lucas wrinkled his brow. "It's a woman's duty. Why should she object?"

Meggie put her hands on her hips and frowned. "You are an oaf, Lucas Kincaid. Things are not the same as they were for us. Men and women have both changed. Their thinking is quite different."

He loved the way her nose wrinkled when she was irritated with him. "Perhaps what men do today might be different from our time, my dear, but what they are thinking is certainly not. And Mr. Grant's thoughts regarding Jessica are precisely the same thoughts I had when I first met you."

In spite of her annoyance at Lucas, Meggie couldn't help but smile. "Every time Dylan stands close to Jessica, I feel something. Almost like a pulse of energy that moves from them into me. Did you feel it, too, Lucas?"

He nodded. "Yes. I feel it. I don't understand it or what it means. But we will soon, my love. Very soon."

Meggie leaned close to Lucas, wanting his nearness even though there could be no physical contact. "Put your arms around me, my darling. Let's pretend, if only for a moment, that we are truly holding each other."

Lucas held out his arms and Meggie moved into them, wishing desperately that Dylan Grant was the answer to their prayers.

"I love you, Lucas," she said quietly.

"And I, you," he answered.

They stood there quietly, pretending it was another time and place. "Lucas," Meggie asked, "do you think Jessica will be angry when she finds out Dylan hasn't been completely truthful with her?"

Lucas smiled. "Of course not. Why would she be angry? She'll understand."

"Do you really think so?"

Lucas smiled reassuringly. "Don't let it bother your pretty little head. Men know about things like this. She'll laugh about it."

But Meggie wasn't so sure, and as she closed her eyes, she prayed that Lucas was right.

Three

Hannibal trotted alongside his mistress while Dylan stayed a few feet behind, listening carefully as Jessica described the town of Makeshift. The wooden sidewalk echoed with the sound of their boot steps, and he made a mental note that the first order of business would be to replace the missing and rotted planks before someone broke a leg.

And speaking of legs, Dylan thought as he scanned Jessica's slender body, she had the kind of legs men dreamed about. They were long and curvy, and the thought of running his hands over her smooth calves and up her thighs brought an ache to his loins. The ache tightened as he watched the sway of her hips.

With a curse, he yanked his gaze from her and stopped to stare through a cracked window of what had once been a general store. Assorted cans and boxes lay toppled on the dusty floor-to-ceiling shelves, and a rusty scale sat on the sales counter. Curtains of spiderwebs draped the entire room.

"I'm surprised you haven't had any vandalism or theft," Dylan said when he spied an antique cash register.

Jessica moved beside him and cupped her eyes to peer through the window. "Few people know about this place. And those who do know better than to bother anything here. I want to renovate this shop and sell items the kids make themselves, plus novelties of the sort tourists go for."

"Tourists?"

A cool breeze picked up at that moment and lifted the ends of Jessica's long hair. She stepped away from the window, and Dylan watched the graceful movement of her fingers as she brushed the loose strands from her face. "You know—" there was a humorous light in her eyes as she looked at him "—that nasty word you've never been accused of. Unfortunately donations and sponsors won't be enough to support Makeshift. We'll have to bring in some commercialism to keep the center going. Anyway, I think it's a good opportunity for the kids to learn about business."

"But why is it so important for you to build your center here?" Dylan asked. "Wouldn't it be easier to set up in town?"

She smiled then. The kind of smile a patient mother gives a child who's asked a silly question. "Easier isn't always best," she said. "I want my kids to be as far away as possible from their everyday lives. They need a place where no one will judge them, a place where they can feel safe."

There had been a fierce protectiveness in Jessica's voice when she'd said "my kids." If she was this devoted to kids she didn't know, Dylan couldn't help but wonder what she'd be like with children of her own. An image of her holding a dark-haired, blue-eyed baby brought a strange ache to his chest, and he quickly shook off the feeling. Hannibal spotted a mouse a few feet down the sidewalk and, with a sharp bark, bounded off after the intruder.

"And what about you?" Dylan asked, watching Hannibal disappear around the building. "Is that why you're here? Because you feel safe?"

She studied him for a long moment, then slipped her hands into her pockets and looked away. "My mother died when I was fourteen," she said quietly. "It devastated me, and I fell into a hole so black and so deep I thought I'd never find my way out. I ran wild, much to my brothers' distress, and I came close to getting into some serious trouble. That's how I ended up working in social services for kids after I graduated from college. I have a group here in town I work with. Right now we only meet on Tuesdays, but after Makeshift is open, we'll have a full-time staff here and bring in kids from all over."

"It's hard to imagine you as a problem teen," Dylan said.

She faced him, tilting her head and smiling slowly. "Because I look so innocent?"

He nodded.

"Looks are deceiving, Dylan. Take you, for instance." She stepped closer to him and her gaze moved over his face. "You aren't nearly as indifferent as you want everyone to believe."

He didn't like the direction this conversation was taking. Nor did he like how close Jessica was standing to him. Close enough to catch the faint scent of jasmine. He felt his pulse begin to pound in his temple, and it took every bit of willpower he possessed not to yank her into his arms and show her that he was far from indifferent when it came to her. "It's dangerous to be so trusting, Jessica."

"I trust you," Jessica said, and watched Dylan's eyes narrow as their gazes meshed. Dangerous was a good word to describe him, she decided. He had a rugged, muscular strength that could intimidate the brawniest of men and make a woman feel light-headed.

When she realized she was actually feeling light-headed herself, she stepped away. "Makeshift will give these teenagers a second chance to get themselves on track again and move in the right direction. Along with general education, we'll teach them job and business skills, too." Hannibal trotted back and she reached down to stroke his fur. "Drafting and construction are viable careers. The center could use someone like you."

His laugh was dry and short. "You've got the wrong man, there. Volunteer and do-gooder weren't listed on my application, nor are they in my vocabulary. You'll have to find someone else for the job."

Was that how he spent his life? Jessica wondered. Moving from job to job, no family, no one to care about him? She couldn't help the tug she felt in her heart for him.

Dylan Grant was becoming more dangerous by the minute, she decided. The thicker the wall he built between them, the more tempted she was to break through it. Hadn't she learned the hard way to keep away from his type? Volunteer and do-gooder weren't the only words missing in Dylan's vocabulary. So were commitment and love and family. And at twenty-seven, she was ready for all three.

But first, she resolved, she had a town to rebuild.

She turned and moved down the sidewalk, pointing out her intentions for each building. The old hotel would be a functioning hotel for tourists and guests. The bank would be the business and accounting office, the tailor shop an arts-and-crafts room. The barbershop would train hairstylists, and the telegraph office would become a computer center.

As Dylan listened to Jessica describe her future town, he was hard put not to catch some of her enthusiasm. It was an impressive undertaking, and he had to admit he admired her dedication. Before he'd come here to Stone Creek and to Makeshift, every job he'd ever worked on had been much the same as the next. Other than the reason that had brought him here, he'd had no cause to think this job would be any different.

But now, as he followed Jessica to the far end of the town, he had the strangest feeling that this job *was* different. Very different. There was something about Makeshift he couldn't put his finger on, something exciting. An energy in the air, in the buildings themselves, that made him feel as if he could do anything.

Except stay of course. That idea was ridiculous. Impossible. He'd tried to settle down once and it had been a disaster. He had no intention of repeating that mistake.

Jessica stopped in front of a small burned-out church at the far end of town. The faded paint had once been white, and half of the steeple was broken off. Mesquite and weeds choked the doors and steps, and a loose shutter rattled in the late-morning breeze. Of all the buildings in Makeshift, the church appeared to have fared the worst.

"I'm not sure where to start here," she said, folding her arms as she stared at the dilapidated building.

"A bulldozer would be my suggestion," Dylan said. "Tear it down and start from scratch."

The light breeze suddenly turned into a cold wind. Dust and leaves flew everywhere. "What the hell . . . ?" Dylan squinted, turning his face from the dirt and debris as he moved up the front steps of the church and struggled to pry loose one of the boards covering the front door. It wouldn't give.

Jessica touched his arm and pulled him away. "The church stays," she said over the noise of the wind and Hannibal's insistent barking. "In fact, it's the first building I want renovated."

When she'd dragged him several yards from the church, the wind calmed to a breeze again. *Weird,* Dylan thought as he slapped at the dust covering his jeans and shirt. "It will cost a lot more to renovate than rebuild," he said. "What difference does it make?"

Her fingers tightened on his arm. "We aren't tearing it down, Dylan."

Jessica's statement went beyond an opinion or recommendation. It was an absolute, emphatic mandate. He looked down at the slender fingers gripping his arm and couldn't help but wonder if the rest of her skin was as smooth and soft. He quickly pushed the thought from his mind.

"Promise me you won't replace even one nail unless it's absolutely necessary," she said earnestly.

The way she was looking at him he would have promised her anything. Her eyes darkened to a smoky, deeper shade of blue, and the unexpected need he felt for her shifted to an ache. But he wasn't the only one affected, he realized. He recognized the desire in her eyes, as well, mixed with surprise. It was like looking into a mirror.

They both stepped away at the same time.

"You're the boss," he said, and heard the strained sound of his voice. "I've seen enough today, anyway. I've got to get back to Cactus Flat and round up a crew."

"How are you going to do that?" she asked with a sigh. "I've already seen what's available."

He smiled. "I've been around this business a few years more than you. I know where to look. I'll set it up and be back tomorrow with my things." He began to head down the street.

"Dylan."

He turned back at the quiet summons. Jessica walked toward him, hands in her pockets, her cheeks bright red.

"There's something I think you should know," she said, staring down at her boots. "Something that might make a difference to your desire to work here."

He didn't want her to say it. If she admitted this physical attraction between them, it would only make things more difficult. If they said nothing, it would be easier to pretend it didn't exist. *Yeah, right.*

"Look, Jessica," he said, "I already know."

"You do?"

He nodded. "And I admit it's pretty intense. But if we just ignore it, it won't get in the way."

She stared at him. "Ignore it?"

"Right."

"You can do that?"

"Sure." He started to feel awkward, discussing it like this.

"It doesn't frighten you?" she asked in amazement.

It scared the hell out of him. But he wasn't ready to admit that, either. "I can deal with it," he said, determined to make himself believe it. "After all, we are both rational mature adults and—"

"Dylan, that's wonderful." She smiled. "Few people even believe in them, let alone accept them."

He was really missing something here. "Accept who?"

"Lucas and Meggie."

"Lucas and Meggie?"

"The ghosts of course. According to the town records, they died in the church fire the night before their wedding. They're still here."

He simply stared at her.

She furrowed her brow. "What did you think I was talking about?"

He shifted uncomfortably. "The ghosts. Right."

"So you don't mind?" she asked.

"Well, I..." *Did he mind?* She'd obviously lost hers. "Let's just say I'm not quite convinced yet."

She smiled slowly. "You stick around, you will be," she said. "But don't worry. You don't bother them and they won't bother you. Right, Hannibal?"

Hannibal barked twice.

"Thanks for the warning," he muttered.

He shook his head, watching as Jessica chased Hannibal back to the hotel. He looked at the church, remembering the strange gust of wind.

Ghosts.

Yeah. Sure.

Never a dull moment, he thought, wondering what other little surprises Jessica Stone had up her sleeve.

If there was one thing Dylan hated more than anything else, it was parties. The first two months he'd been married he'd been forced into an endless stream of socializing with people he didn't know, and certainly didn't care about. He'd never been one for idle conversation, and from his experience, the talk at family gatherings was as idle as it came.

He should have known that the Stone family would not fit that mold.

The second he'd stepped into Jake's house he felt as if he'd been whisked into a tornado. Three little girls ran past, shrieking, and when Jessica called to one of them, a dark-haired child ran back and hugged her. Dylan was stunned at the resemblance between them.

"Dylan, this is my half sister, Emma," Jessica said. "Emma, this is Dylan Grant."

The child smiled, then ran off to join the other two girls. From then on, Dylan was busy shaking hands and trying to remember names. Savannah, Jake's wife, was a blonde with iridescent green eyes and a soft Southern drawl. Annie, Jared's fiancée, was also a blonde, with expressive hazel eyes and the glow of a woman about to be married to a man she loved.

Dylan felt a tug of envy, wondering what it would be like to see that look on a woman's face for him. When Dylan shook Jared's hand and congratulated him, Jared nodded stiffly. When Dylan glanced at Jessica, he saw her frown at her brother.

Then there were neighbors and friends. A giant of a man named Hugh Slater, who was Jared's foreman on his oil rig. A crusty older man named Digger who didn't speak—he boomed. And a neighboring rancher, Sam McCants, who smiled politely as they shook hands, but never took his eyes off Jessica.

Not that he blamed the man, Dylan thought. Jessica looked radiant tonight. She had on a deep blue long cotton dress that clung to her curves. The scooped neckline revealed the soft swell of her breasts, but was not so suggestive as to show cleavage. When he'd offered to drive her truck here tonight and he'd helped her into the cab, a brief flash of one long leg had elevated his body temperature several degrees.

Dylan felt his body tighten when Sam put an arm around Jessica and kissed her on the lips. It wasn't a long kiss, and it certainly wasn't passionate, but Dylan decided he didn't like the man.

"So, Dylan," Sam said, his arm still draped around Jessica, "why don't you tell us your secret?"

Dylan hesitated. He had the strangest feeling everyone had quieted and was listening for his answer. Jake and Jared watched him intently. "Secret?"

"I understand you're staying at Makeshift," Sam said good-naturedly. "I've been trying for years to get around Jake and Jared where Jessica is concerned, with no luck. So what's your secret?"

Jessica blushed and slipped out from Sam's hold. "You're incorrigible, Sam McCants. Room and board is part of Dylan's pay. It's as simple as that."

"Room *and* board?" Jake raised one eyebrow and looked at Dylan first, then Jessica. "You mean you're going to *cook,* too?"

Jessica ground her teeth. She hadn't intended to mention that fact. Her brothers would never let her live it down. She flashed Dylan a scathing look. He smiled back.

"Dylan's managed to put together a crew already," Jessica said, hoping to change the subject. "We'll be starting tomorrow."

Jared eyed Dylan. "You're a fast worker."

"I don't believe in wasting time," Dylan returned.

Jessica was going to kill Jared. Slowly and painfully. He'd been rude from the minute they'd walked in. When were her brothers ever going to learn she wasn't a child anymore?

Smiling brightly, Savannah stepped between the two men and pressed a beer into Dylan's hand. "So has Jessica told you about her ghosts yet?" she asked.

Dylan thanked Savannah and turned his gaze to Jessica as he took a long swig of the beer. "She mentioned them."

"We think it's romantic," Annie said. "The idea of two souls so in love they refuse to leave the town where they were to be married."

Dylan still couldn't believe that Jessica actually believed this crazy idea. He wondered if she was putting him on, trying to get back at him for the room-and-board business. He glanced at her, and she smiled sweetly.

"Hello, everyone," a woman's high-pitched voice interrupted the conversation. The room went silent, and all heads turned in the direction of the front door.

Dylan watched as an attractive woman of about fifty moved into the room. The red in her plaid jacket nearly matched the red of her swept-up hair, and her black velvet skirt matched her shoes. An older man in an expensive blue suit followed the woman into the room. Dylan noticed the man's pallor was as gray as his hair.

"So sorry we're late," the woman said, though Dylan had the feeling that no one in the room had been particularly lamenting that fact. "It was a battle to drag Daddy away from one of his business calls. I swear, he's been locked up in the study half the day."

The woman brushed a kiss first on Jake's cheek, then Jared's. It was tolerated more than welcomed, Dylan noticed.

The woman hugged Jessica, then settled her gaze on Dylan. "Oh, Jessica, dear, is this the young man who's staying with you in that town of yours?"

Jessica flinched, then forced a smile. "He's not *staying* with me, Myrna. He's the foreman I've hired to renovate Makeshift. Dylan Grant, this is Myrna Stone, my step-mother, and her father, Carlton Hewitt."

Carlton's grip was firm, Dylan noted, though his palm was cold. Myrna's grip was as weak as it was brief.

"I've tried everything to dissuade Jessica from this ridiculous undertaking, but she simply won't listen," Myrna said with exasperation. "She could have built three centers somewhere else with the money I've offered her for that land. I'm sure you agree, Mr. Grant, that on a financial level, the entire project is preposterous."

Though it was subtle, Dylan noticed that Jake and Jared had moved closer to Jessica in a protective gesture. Strange, he thought, but the minute Myrna had walked into the room, Dylan had instinctively moved closer himself.

"On a financial level, I don't agree at all," Dylan said dryly. "I wouldn't have a job if it wasn't for Makeshift, would I?" He smiled and raised his bottle to her.

Myrna frowned at him and sniffed piously. "It's a common fact that all these problem children are from lower-class families who expect everything to be handed to them on a silver platter."

Dylan was prepared to respond to the woman's stupid remark, but Jessica didn't give him time. Eyes narrowed, she faced her stepmother.

"Myrna," she said, her patience barely controlled, "there are no 'common facts' when it comes to problems in a home, nor are problems particular to any one class. The kids who come to me aren't asking for any favors, just a break. And from my experience, the only people who expect anything handed to them on a silver platter are those who already own one."

Carlton laid a hand on his daughter's arm. "Jessica's right, Myrna. I'm sure her center will help a great many young men and women."

Myrna, oblivious to Jessica's sarcasm and her father's attempt to smooth over the conversation, kept right on. "And the community here is none too happy about encouraging these juvenile delinquents, Jessica."

"The *community*," Jessica said tightly, "consists of more people than a few close-minded ignorant individuals. The people of Cactus Flat and all the neighboring ranches have more than proved their support."

Myrna's chin lifted at Jessica's affront. Jessica's eyes glinted with purpose, and Dylan struggled to hold back a smile. Myrna was the one who needed protection here, he realized, not Jessica.

"Myrna—" Carlton stepped beside his daughter and smiled "—why don't you go find me a drink, dear? My throat's a little dry."

"It's all that medication you take," Myrna said sternly, shifting easily from one lecture to another. "I really do think you should speak to your doctor. I swear, in the month you've been staying with me, you could have bought Cactus Flat Pharmacy with the prescriptions you've purchased."

"Why don't we all have a drink?" Savannah interjected smoothly before Myrna could continue. "I believe it's time for a toast to the future bride and groom."

Glasses were raised, refilled and raised several times as an endless stream of good wishes were made. Some were humorous, some were emotional, but they were all sincere.

If possible, Dylan would have made an exit. He didn't fit in where a celebration of marriage was concerned. He saw the looks exchanged not only between Jared and Annie, but between Jake and Savannah, too, and he felt as if his clothes were suddenly too tight.

When Jessica leaned close and touched his arm, he nearly jumped at the contact.

"Relax, Dylan," she said with a laugh. "Marriage isn't contagious. I just thought you might like to add a toast of your own."

He didn't have a clue what to say. He simply shook his head, stunned that she would even think to include him in the festivities. His entire life he'd been on the outside looking in, wondering what a "normal" family was like. At thirty-four, it was still a mystery. A mystery he had no delusions about solving.

Jessica was grateful when Dylan offered to drive back to Makeshift after the party. With a soft moan, she kicked off her high heels and settled back against the pickup's passenger seat. The headlights stretched out on the dark road ahead of them, and a cool breeze floated through the cab.

"So tell me the truth." She tucked her legs beneath her. "What do you think?"

He glanced over at her. "Nice legs."

She frowned at him and pulled her dress over the limb she'd exposed. "You know what I mean. My family. What do you think of them?"

"Emma's going to break a few hearts one of these days."

Jessica smiled. "She is, isn't she?"

"She looks exactly like you."

Dylan glanced at her again, and she felt a wave of heat spread through her body. She was glad it was too dark for him to see the blush on her cheeks.

"You mentioned she was your half sister," Dylan said.

She nodded. "It's complicated, but after my mother died, my father married Myrna out of loneliness. Shortly afterward, he met another woman, Angela, and truly fell in love. He was going to divorce Myrna, but Angela left one day without a word. J.T., my father, was heartbroken, but it was years before he decided to look for her. He hired a private investigator to find Angela, and it was then that Emma's birth records were discovered."

Dylan had one hand on the wheel, the other resting on the open cab window. Jessica watched the wind ruffle his dark hair.

"And Angela?" Dylan slowed the truck and turned onto the dirt road to Makeshift. "Did he find her?"

Jessica shook her head. "Jake continued the search after J.T.'s death and found Emma, but Angela had died in a small plane crash a few months earlier. Emma was living with her aunt in Georgia. And her aunt just happens to be—"

"Savannah," he finished.

She smiled. "Right. She and Jake have only been married two months."

That was two months too long in Dylan's book, but he kept quiet. Besides, he liked the sound of Jessica's voice when she talked about her family. Sort of soft and dreamy. "And now Jared and Annie."

Her smile broadened. "That's even more incredible. Annie was engaged to my brother Jonathan, Jared's twin. He died four years ago in an oil-rig accident here at Stone Creek. Jared blamed himself and took off for South America. When my father died, Jared came back and reopened the well. Annie showed up as a geologist hired by the company backing Jared."

"And the rest," Dylan said, "is history, right?"

"Right." She grinned at him, then held on as the truck bounced over a bump. "You were in South America, weren't you?"

"For a while." Dylan focused on the road. "And then there's Myrna," he said.

"Oh, yes." Jessica sighed. "We certainly can't forget Myrna, can we?"

Dylan once again glanced at Jessica as she lifted her hair off her neck. The moonlight glowed softly on her creamy skin, and as she raised her arms, her breasts lifted enticingly. He looked quickly away.

"Why does she want your land?" he asked, keeping the conversation on Jessica's stepmother. That was certain to cool his blood.

"Myrna spent all my father's money building a huge house—Stone Manor—in the middle of Stone Creek. He left her the house, but no land. She gave up hounding Jake and Jared to sell her their property and started in on me."

"What's she want it for?"

"She has this crazy idea she wants to build stables and raise Thoroughbreds. Her father has bought her everything she's ever wanted in her entire life. This is the first time anyone has said no to the woman. It's driving her crazy."

Dylan grinned. "Do I sense a perverse pleasure here?"

Jessica laughed and the sound enchanted Dylan. "Intensely perverse," she said with a wicked grin.

"And her father," Dylan asked, "he's not well, is he?"

Jessica nodded grimly. "Carlton has never talked about it, but everyone can see how ill he's become in the past few weeks since he's been staying with her. Everyone except Myrna of course. She's in complete denial that her father is not the same man he once was."

Dylan parked the truck in front of the hotel. He came around and opened the door for Jessica. She slid out, heels in her hand, but when one of her stockinged feet landed on a rock, she winced and stumbled. He reached out and put his hands on her waist to steady her.

He stood there, looking down at her, his long fingers still circling her waist. The half-moon was bright enough for Jessica to see Dylan's eyes narrow and his mouth tighten. She was certain her heart stopped for an instant, then leapt into double time. She became infinitely aware that the thin fabric of her dress was all that separated bare skin from bare skin.

The air seemed to thicken and grow still. Shadows closed in around them, and it almost felt as if Makeshift were holding its breath, waiting. Jessica knew *she* was.

He released her slowly.

"Dylan," she said when she managed to find her voice, "I, uh, want to apologize for Jared's behavior tonight."

"Jared?"

"He was rude to you. I'm sorry. Both Jake and Jared have been watching over me for so long they just don't know when to quit."

"They weren't the only ones watching you tonight."

Pulse pounding, she looked up at him. "Oh?"

He shook his head. "Sam couldn't take his eyes off you."

It took a moment for his words to sink in. Disappointment cut into her, then amazement. "Sam? Watching me?"

"Like a hawk."

"You mean you think *Sam* is interested in *me?*"

She started to laugh. Dylan watched her, his expression tight.

"Dylan—" she couldn't stop laughing, even though she realized he was getting angry "—I think I know when a man is attracted to me. There's nothing between Sam and me."

"I suppose that kiss he gave you was nothing, also." Why had he started this conversation? he wondered irritably. And why couldn't he let it drop?

Her eyes sparkled with tears of laughter. "You are really beginning to sound like my brothers, Dylan."

He didn't like being compared to her brothers. "Maybe your brothers aren't so wrong. Maybe you are naive and you do need protection."

"Protection? Out here?" She threw her arms out in disbelief and started to laugh again. "You're crazy. What in the world would I need protection from?"

The laughter was still on her lips as he grabbed her to him and covered her mouth with his. He heard, as well as felt, her sharp intake of air.

She tasted like no other woman. Intoxicating. Exciting. The passion shimmered between them, and he ground his mouth against hers. Her lips parted and he explored the sweetness of her with his tongue. She met him, tentatively at first, then dropped her shoes to the ground, slid her arms around his shoulders and rose on tiptoe.

Intense pleasure, as well as shock, coursed through Jessica. She clung to Dylan, shocked by her brazen response to his kiss. This was like nothing she'd ever experienced before. Her bones felt as if they were melting. Her heart raced. An inexplicable tightness knotted and unknotted in her belly. His large hands cupped her bottom and pulled her fully against his arousal. She moaned softly, needing to be closer still.

Suddenly he released her, and she stumbled back against the cab of the truck. Confused, she stared at him, her breathing heavy and uneven. His face was hard as he stared back; his eyes glinted fiercely.

"That's what you need protection from," he said darkly. "Men like me."

Dylan turned and walked away, knowing that if he looked back there'd be nothing on this earth that could stop him from taking this woman to his bed.

But Jessica wasn't a one-night woman. She deserved much better than that. She sure deserved better than him.

He kept walking, away from the hotel, away from her, and didn't stop until he reached the barn at the far edge of town. He drew in a deep breath, letting his blood cool as he raked his hands through his hair. Then he went very still.

Someone was watching him. He knew it. Slowly he turned and stared into the dark shadows in the barn.

One of them moved toward him. Out of the barn and into the moonlight.

It was Jared.

The two men looked at each other for a long moment.

"Well, that was certainly something I never thought I'd see," Jared said.

Guilt held Dylan speechless as he stared at Jared.

"I mean, who would have ever thought, Dylan Grant, at my engagement party."

Dylan let out the breath he'd been holding.

A slow grin started on Jared. Dylan grinned back.

"Nice to see you again, buddy," Jared said.

"Likewise," Dylan returned.

With a small laugh, they shook hands and slapped their arms around each other.

Four

Jared stepped back, and the moon cast long eerie shadows into the darkness. "Where's Jessica?" he asked quietly, glancing over Dylan's shoulder.

Probably extensively cursing the name Dylan Grant. "She went to bed. I just thought I'd check things out around town before I turned in."

"And that dog of hers?"

"She keeps Hannibal inside with her at night."

Jared looked around cautiously, making sure they were alone, then faced Dylan again. "Thanks for coming."

Both men knew that thanks weren't necessary. They'd been through too much together. "I'd seen enough Venezuelan jungles to last me awhile, anyway. It was time to come back to the States."

Not home, Dylan thought. He'd never had a place he'd ever thought of as home. "Besides—" he grinned "—I had to meet the woman that tamed the infamous Jared Stone.

Now that I have, I can't figure out what an incredible lady like Annie is doing with the likes of you."

"I haven't figured it out myself, pal." Jared's face softened as he looked at Dylan. "We're having a baby next June."

An old hurt threatened to surface, but Dylan forced it down. He wouldn't let his past take away from the pleasure of his friend's happiness. "The first of many, I hope," Dylan said, and shook Jared's hand again.

Both Dylan and Jared tensed at the hoot of a barn owl, then laughed softly and moved around the corner of the barn into the shadows. Jared's truck was parked a few feet away, out of sight of the hotel.

Propping one boot against an old wooden water trough, Jared folded his arms and leaned back against the weathered barn. "So what do you think of Jess?"

Dylan thought it best not to go with the first answer that came to mind. He wanted to wear his teeth, not carry them. "I think she's going to be mighty ticked off if she finds out you and Jake asked me to come here and take this job so I could keep an eye on her."

"So she doesn't suspect anything?"

Dylan shook his head. "You almost had me convinced you didn't know me when she introduced us yesterday. She thinks Jake invited me tonight so the two of you could interrogate me further."

"I laid it on a little thick," Jared admitted. "But if I hadn't, Jess would've wondered."

"She asked me about South America tonight," Dylan said. "There was a spark of connection in her eyes."

Jared frowned. "We'll just have to be careful. Even Annie's been watching me as if she thinks something's up."

"She doesn't know about any of this?"

Jared gave a snort of laughter. "I couldn't tell Annie any more than Jake could tell Savannah. These women hang together. They might think it was deceitful."

Dylan couldn't help but grin. "It *is* deceitful."

Jared shrugged. "But necessary. Jessica's too damn trusting. She wouldn't know a bad guy if he stuck a sign on his forehead and introduced himself."

Like me, Dylan thought. He'd given her a good example of a bad guy himself tonight, and the thought left him with a sour taste. "Why don't you tell me exactly what's going on here?"

Jared hunkered down and picked up a small piece of splintered wood, then drew a rectangle in the dirt. "Stone Creek is about one hundred thousand acres. This is Jessica's land, mine is east of here—" he divided the rectangle into smaller boxes "—Jake's is north, and Emma's is east of Jake's. Myrna's house sits smack-dab in the middle."

"Jessica told me your father left Myrna no land."

Jared nodded. "She's been trying to buy our land since the will was read. First Jake's, then mine. We both had strange accidents, potentially tragic. We caught the guy responsible for Jake's problems. He's in jail, but refuses to implicate anyone else. We suspect he's been paid well enough by someone else to do the time. The man who tried to sabotage my rig got away before we could question him."

"You think he'll be back?"

"No. But I think whoever hired these guys will try something with Jessica. She's an easy target out here by herself."

"Do you think Myrna's involved?"

Jared sighed. "I don't know. My stepmother has done a lot of selfish things, but it's hard to believe she'd go this far or actually hurt anyone."

"So who, other than Myrna, would gain from this land?"

"It's good ranch land. I struck oil a few weeks ago. Jessica's parcel is closest to the highway, and there's been some talk of an airport being built west of here somewhere."

"So just about everyone," Dylan said, shaking his head. "And Sam? Stone Creek land would be valuable to a neighboring ranch."

"Sam would never hurt Jessica," Jared said. "He's crazy about her."

A knot of irritation tightened in Dylan's stomach. He refused to allow himself to think about the rancher and Jessica. He'd gotten in enough trouble with that already tonight. "Myrna mentioned there were some people in Cactus Flat opposed to Jessica's youth center. Are you expecting trouble there?"

"I don't know." Jared tossed down the stick and stood. "Just keep your eyes open, pal. It could be anybody."

Dylan nodded grimly and straightened.

"We're also going to have to be careful that Jessica doesn't find out about our arrangement," Jared added. "Annie and Savannah will be widows, and Lord only knows what she'll do to you."

Considering Jessica's imagination, her retribution was a scary thought, Dylan decided. "We'll just have to make sure she doesn't find out, then, won't we?"

Jared nodded. "Thanks again for coming, Dylan. There's no one I trust more than you to take care of my little sister."

"I think I can survive a few weeks in a ghost town," Dylan said. "I'd be rotting in a South American prison if it wasn't for you."

Grim-faced, Jared shook his head. "That was a raw deal you got. Everyone on that rig knew it was the operations manager who killed that girl in the hit-and-run."

"But you were the only one who did anything about it." Dylan looked at Jared. "You could have lost your job, too, or even ended up in the cell next to mine."

"I didn't give a damn about the job, and there was no jail worse than the one I put myself in after my brother died and I'd convinced myself I could never be with Annie," Jared said quietly. "But now that we're together and the baby is coming, I sure am glad that you and I both got out of there."

They were quiet for a moment, remembering. It was a past neither man wanted to dwell on.

"Speaking of getting out—" Jared looked around "—I'd better go. If Jessie sees us, that jail cell might not look so bad, after all."

They said good-night, then Jared got into his truck and drove away. Dylan watched the taillights until they disappeared into the night, then turned and started back to the hotel. He thought of Jessica there, lying in bed, her long slender body stretched across the sheets. His hands and throat tightened at the image.

Jared's words echoed in Dylan's mind. *There's no one I trust more than you to take care of my little sister.*

Didn't Jared realize that his "little sister" was a full-grown woman? A damn sexy one. He had to know that any man would want to take Jessica to bed.

Of course he knew, Dylan thought with a heavy sigh. That was why Jared had called him. Because he trusted him, not only to keep Jessica safe, but to keep his distance. And Dylan knew he'd already betrayed that trust.

He stared up at the brilliant half-moon overhead. He heard the lonely howl of a coyote, and the scent of mesquite filled the cool night air.

And suddenly the stifling humidity and primitive conditions of the mosquito-infested jungles of South America were damn appealing.

Jessica was checking on a tray of biscuits in the oven of the hotel's antique cast-iron wood-burning stove when Dylan finally made his appearance the next morning. Hannibal jumped up from the corner he'd settled into and padded over to greet him.

Traitor, she thought, watching as Hannibal wagged his tail. She glanced casually at Dylan, noting that his dark hair was slicked back, still damp from the shower, his clean denim shirt rolled to the elbows. He hadn't shaved, and the rugged look, combined with his jeans and work boots, was pure male.

Her heart skipped and she swore silently. She was tired and stressed and cranky as hell, but she was also determined not to let the man know he had even the slightest effect on her.

His expression was one of amazement as he stood in the doorway and glanced around the kitchen. She'd been up cleaning the room since well before dawn. After five hours of tossing and turning, she'd needed something to do. The hardwood floors were swept clean, the butcher-block counters and iron sink spotless.

"Mornin'," he said.

It was a cautious greeting. *Good,* she thought. After the way he'd kissed her, then left her standing alone last night, he'd better be cautious. She hated the fact that even now her knees were weak and her hands were trembling. "Morning."

He moved slowly into the room, obviously testing the waters. "Is that bacon or sausage I smell?"

She shut the oven door, but kept the pot holder in her hand so she'd have something to hold on to. "Both."

Both? Dylan couldn't believe it. How angry could Jessica be with him if she'd prepared such a lavish breakfast? If anything, he'd expected a cool nod as she handed him his walking papers.

Could he have misread her response to him last night? he wondered. She'd clung to him, as eager for him as he was for her. All night he kept hearing that soft little moan of hers. Needless to say, it had been a hard night.

He watched her calmly pour a cup of steaming coffee into a mug. Maybe the kiss hadn't meant anything to her, after all, he thought with more irritation than he understood. Hell, if she could dismiss it so easily, then so could he. It was nothing. A simple kiss. No big deal.

Okay, so fine. It certainly made life easier. He was glad that Jessica was a woman who didn't overreact. Now he could enjoy his breakfast and forget about last night. Good.

"Sugar?"

He glanced at her. "Excuse me?"

"You want sugar or cream?" she asked.

"Oh." He shook his head. "No. Just black, thanks."

She set the coffee on the table and gestured for him to sit. She'd pulled her hair into a ponytail, but several strands had pulled loose and circled her flour-smudged heart-shaped face. The white chef's apron she wore over her jeans and blue plaid shirt looked as if she'd been cooking for a week.

Unbidden, desire flared, and he quickly shoved it back down. It wasn't as if she was wearing silk or lace, for God's sake, but he still couldn't remember when a woman had ever looked sexier.

"You got this old stove working by yourself?" he asked, forcing his mind in another direction.

Jessica turned back to the stove. "After I cleaned out the chimney flue and found some firewood."

She must have been up hours ago to have accomplished all she had and fixed breakfast, also. He felt a pang of guilt for forcing her into cooking, but tamped down the feeling when his stomach growled. After all, a man had to eat. And the incredible aromas of bacon, fresh-baked biscuits and coffee had his mouth watering already.

He noticed she had only one place set. "You aren't eating?"

She took the biscuits out of the oven and set them on the table, then lifted a cast-iron frying pan off the stove and moved beside him. "I don't normally eat breakfast. Eggs?"

He smiled broadly. "Thanks."

She scooped up a ladleful and slapped it on his plate.

His smile froze as he stared at the unrecognizable yellow and gray lumps.

"They started off fried," she said, "went to scrambled and ended up foozled."

His smile began to fade. "Foozled?"

"Foozled. You know, whatever."

He watched as she dropped something dark brown and round beside the eggs. It hit the plate like a rock. In fact, Dylan thought, it *looked* like a rock. What he thought might be bacon came next, but there were too many small black pieces to be sure.

"I haven't quite gotten used to the temperature control," she said casually. "But for my first attempt, I think it's pretty good."

Pretty good? She wasn't serious. She couldn't be. She waved a hand at him. "Go on," she said, "don't be shy."

He decided to start with a biscuit. They looked safe, anyway. He reached for one. It was hot and steaming as he took a bite.

And nearly broke a tooth.

"I burned the first two batches," she said. "I guess the third time's a charm."

He managed to gnaw off a small bite. It had all the charm and chewability of a fence post. "Something wrong?" she asked sweetly as he attempted to chew.

He shook his head and reached for his coffee. The hot liquid might soak the hard chunk in his mouth enough so he could swallow. He took a sip, then froze.

Mistake. Big mistake.

Mouth full, unable to speak, he narrowed his eyes and stared at Jessica. She stared back innocently.

Enough was enough.

Jessica saw the fury building in Dylan's eyes, but she was having too much fun to care. Cheeks puffed out, he slammed both hands on the table and stood. She moved out of the way when he walked to the counter. She bit the side of her mouth to keep from laughing when he spit the coffee and biscuit into the sink.

"Really, Dylan." She folded her arms. "You don't have to be so rude."

He reached for a cup in the cupboard and poured water into it from a carafe of water sitting on the counter. He rinsed his mouth and spit again, grounds filling the sink.

"My survival depended on it," he returned sharply, spitting several more times.

"It was a little strong, I admit, but you're exaggerating."

"I've seen tar pits that weren't as thick as what I just drank." He wiped his mouth on a napkin and grimaced.

She was loving every minute of this. Dylan, however, was growing angrier by the minute. "I'll get better, I'm sure. A little practice is all I need."

"Not on me, you don't. You've done enough experimenting for one day." He stalked over to her, his gaze leveled dangerously on her. "Or maybe this is payback for last night, Jessica," he said deeply.

Her heart began to thud heavily against her ribs. She lifted her chin, refusing to back down from his steady gaze. "I haven't a clue what you're talking about."

"Really?" He leaned close and she caught the scent of him, a mixture of soap and man. Her chest felt tight. Her skin felt tight.

"Maybe that kiss rattled you more than you want to admit," he said, "so you decided to poison me."

Dylan's eyes darkened and he moved closer still. She held her breath, angry with herself because she wanted him to touch her as much as she wanted him to pull away.

He stopped within inches of her, then reached around her, grabbed a biscuit and threw it to Hannibal. The dog picked it up, tossed it around in his jaws a few times, then dropped it back on the floor with a clunk.

She lifted a brow. "Don't say one word, Dylan. Not one."

He smiled slowly and moved toward the doorway. "The only thing I can say about those biscuits is that I sure as hell wouldn't want to get hit with one."

"Dylan."

He stopped and turned.

The first biscuit caught him square in the chest, the second glanced off his arm. Eyes glinting, he started back toward her, but Hannibal intervened with a warning bark. Jessica smiled smugly.

Stomach growling, Dylan clenched his fists, then turned and left, wondering if that bag of chocolate-chip cookies he'd bought in town was still in his duffel bag.

By the end of that same day, Makeshift's transformation had begun.

The crew had arrived shortly after the biscuit-throwing incident, and after a brief orientation, Dylan assigned the men their tasks. As Jessica had insisted, Dylan started work on the church first. Six of the eight men ripped down boards and carted trash to a central pile beside the barn, while the other two followed Dylan back to the hotel to work on the wiring. Jessica kept busy salvaging a good portion of what the men were tossing out, determined that not one original nail or screw be thrown away.

Dylan had reappeared at the noon break, but when she offered to make him a sandwich, he frowned and waved her off, telling her he had to go into town for supplies and wouldn't be back until much later in the day, *after* he had dinner in town, he added dryly. She felt a twinge of guilt, but was too tired and too busy to discuss the issue. *Be that way,* she said silently as she watched him drive away in her pickup. She had more things on her mind right now than a hot-tempered cantankerous male.

But now that the crew had all left and the sun had begun its slow descent, Jessica sank into the back church pews that had been salvaged and found she couldn't do anything *but* think about that hot-tempered cantankerous male and wonder when he'd return.

Closing her eyes, she settled back on the hard oak seat and sighed. Hannibal curled beside her and sighed, too. After a long busy day investigating all the strangers, the dog was as exhausted as his mistress.

Jessica was used to being alone in Makeshift. She'd never wanted anyone else here. So why, then, did she feel such a strange sense of loneliness, and how could she suddenly be anxious for someone to be here with her?

And it wasn't just anyone, she acknowledged reluctantly. It was Dylan.

It was crazy. She barely knew the man. And what she knew of him should make her *not* want to know him, at least not beyond anything of a professional nature. Settling down wasn't in the man's profile.

She thought of the kiss they'd shared and couldn't stop the shiver that passed through her. No one had ever kissed her like that before, or at least she'd never responded to anyone like that before, not even to Bob, her one and only love affair after she'd graduated from college. He'd been another counselor at the Dallas-based youth center where she worked. It hadn't taken Jessica long to realize that Bob had more problems than the kids, only he wasn't looking for help; he was looking for a live-in maid.

Sort of like Dylan, she thought with a frown.

She couldn't stop smiling as she remembered the expression on his face when she'd served him that horrible breakfast. She'd felt almost sorry for him. Almost.

Eyes still closed, she forced Dylan from her mind and focused on the church. Makeshift was the most important thing to her. Bringing her dream to life was all that mattered.

She ran her fingers over the smooth worn wood of the pew, wondering how many people had sat right here where she was. Her ancestors, all the townspeople, what it must have looked like on a Sunday morning...

She could almost hear the steady clang-clang of the church bell, a choir singing "Amazing Grace," greetings exchanged between the patrons and the whine of a child as his mother tugged his ear to sit still. The loving exchange between a couple about to be married...

"One week, my love. In this very church we'll say our vows and you'll be my wife forever."

"And you my husband. Forever."

Jessica smiled as she watched the man and woman in her daydream steal a kiss. They were so clear in her mind, as were the sights and sounds.

And the smells. A delicious aroma wafted through her senses, so real it made her stomach growl and her mouth water. So real she breathed in deeply to capture the heavenly scent of—

Hamburgers.

Her eyes flew open. Dylan stood beside her, his gaze intent as he watched her. He carried a brown paper bag in his hand.

"Did I wake you?" he asked.

"Of course not," she said curtly, irritated that he'd managed to sneak up on her like that. She glanced at Hannibal and frowned. Her watchdog was turning into a "come-on-in-and-don't-mind-me" dog. At the smell of food, though, the animal lifted his head and sniffed the air. "I'm just trying to imagine what it was like to live here more than a hundred years ago."

"Why don't you just ask your ghosts?"

She lifted a brow. "Is that sarcasm I hear in your voice?"

"Me? Sarcastic?" He grinned and sat down next to her.

Food had obviously improved his mood, Jessica noted, and felt relieved he wasn't still angry about the breakfast. She was also glad he placed the paper bag on the seat between them. She needed whatever barrier she could find between herself and Dylan. The smells from the bag, however, were driving her nearly as crazy as the man.

"For your information," she said with a lift of her chin, "the ghosts here are real."

The bag crackled as Dylan rummaged through it. He pulled out a paper-wrapped hamburger and handed it to her.

She shook her head stubbornly. "I was planning a stew. I found a recipe in an old cookbook."

He pressed the hamburger in her hand. "Toss it in the trash with those biscuits."

Hunger overrode her pride. She took a bite and sighed with pleasure as she settled back and glanced at the bag. "Please tell me you have fries in there."

"Catsup, too."

She dug in the bag and popped a fry into her mouth. "You are too good to be true, Dylan Grant."

He looked away from her, and his glance assessed the work done that day. The crew had removed the debris and the worst of the burned pews; the boarded-up windows were open, but had no glass. There was an airy, reverent feeling inside the church, and Jessica felt herself relaxing. Dylan broke off a piece of his hamburger and tossed it to Hannibal, then he, too, settled back to eat. "Tell me about your ghosts."

"They aren't *my* ghosts." She rarely talked about them. No one believed her, so what was the point? Her family humored her on the subject, as she knew Dylan was doing now. Still, it made no difference to her what Dylan did or didn't believe.

"Have you seen them?" he asked.

He handed her a packet of catsup, and the amusement she saw in his eyes made her spine stiffen. "I *hear* them," she said. "Sometimes just a word or two, other times more."

There *was* more, Jessica thought. A great deal more. But she'd never shared that with anyone, and she certainly didn't intend to start with Dylan of all people. He wouldn't believe it. Sometimes she wasn't sure even she believed it.

Dylan didn't believe a word of what Jessica was saying of course, but he certainly enjoyed listening to her. And the expression on her face and the way her blue eyes shone as she talked about her spirits captivated him. He wouldn't care if she wanted to talk about quilt making. "So you've never seen them," he said. "You just hear them."

"That's right."

He chewed thoughtfully. "Didn't you say you knew their names?"

"Meggie and Lucas. Meggie was the schoolmarm, and Lucas owned the saloon."

"Meggie and Lucas," he repeated. "Nice names." The shadows deepened and a cool breeze flowed over them. Dylan watched one loose strand of hair curl around Jessica's cheek. Instinctively he reached out and tucked it behind her ear. "Were they lovers?"

Lovers. The word hovered between them. His touch was no more than the brush of his finger on her cheek, yet desire flared with an intensity that startled him. Her lips were close. Close and tempting.

Jessica had gone still at his touch. "Does it matter?"

He smiled. "Probably to them it did."

The air grew heavy and thick, as if a storm was coming. The cool breeze turned to a warm wind.

Jessica leaned closer, her expression intense. "Dylan, didn't you ever feel something, something you couldn't see and yet the feeling was too strong to deny it existed? Something you knew to be true, despite all reason and logic?"

He was feeling it now. With her. A need beyond all reason. A desire beyond logic. A flood of sensation that had nothing to do with ghosts or spirits, unless he counted spirits of the flesh.

The need to touch her overwhelmed him, and it took every ounce of willpower he possessed to move away from her before he did something foolish again. It had been a mistake to kiss her last night. He knew what she tasted like now, how her body felt pressed against his.

He wanted desperately to kiss her again. Now. To drag her against him right here. He felt a sudden rush of anger. At himself, at the situation. He was supposed to keep an eye on Jessica, dammit, not seduce her.

"There's nothing more than what we see, Jessica," he said quietly. "And sometimes even that's a lie."

He stood, jamming his hands into his pockets. "I'll be working on the blueprints for the next few nights. Unless it's important, I'd rather you didn't disturb me."

She looked at him, her gaze suddenly cool. "I wouldn't dream of disturbing you, Dylan."

It was all he could do not to laugh. If she had any idea just exactly how much she did disturb him, the laugh would be hers alone. Jaw tight, he walked away on feet that felt like lead.

"It's truly happening, Lucas," Meggie whispered, careful not to let Jessica hear. "After one hundred and twenty years our church is going to be restored."

Lucas watched Meggie as she stood smiling at the altar rail, her eyes bright as she surveyed the work done that day. She'd been on the original building committee, and the church was as precious to her as if it were her own child.

Lucas turned away. Even after all this time, he still felt anger whenever he came here—rage that he couldn't stop the fire, that he hadn't saved Meggie.

She moved beside him and lifted her sad gaze to his. "You never should have come into the church that night, Lucas," she said quietly, understanding what he was feeling. "We didn't both have to die."

He turned sharply to her, lifting his hands in a futile gesture to touch her. "My life ended the moment I knew you

were trapped in here," he said hoarsely. *"I never would have
left you alone."*

*Meggie lifted her fingers to her lips, then pressed her hand
close to his mouth. "My only regret is that I never became
your wife."*

"You are my wife," Lucas insisted. *"In my heart and in
my soul."*

*She shook her head. "The vows were not exchanged here
in God's church."*

*Frustration filled Lucas. It was impossible to discuss it
with Meggie. He'd never been able to convince her that the
betrothal made no difference to him. Following the fire, the
town moved services into the town hall. Meggie's beloved
church had never been rebuilt.*

Until now.

*Meggie and Lucas watched as Jessica rose from the pew
where she'd been sitting and gathered up the food wrapping. She glanced around the church, then turned and left.*

"She's troubled by her feelings for Dylan," Meggie said,
*then sighed deeply. "He doesn't believe we exist, Lucas. I
was so sure he was the one, but if he doesn't believe, he can't
be."*

*"I seem to recall even we needed some time to accept the
reality of our existence, my sweet." He smiled. "Or should
I say, lack of?"*

*She smiled back. "It was strange, wasn't it? Being so
frightened, then peaceful. It felt like a dream."*

*A dream, Lucas thought. One where he never slept and
never woke. And always the feeling that he needed to move
on.*

*But he wouldn't leave Meggie. Not ever. And she wouldn't
leave Makeshift.*

*So here they were. And unless something happened soon,
Lucas had the sinking feeling they always would be.*

Five

It took Jessica the next four days to strip bare the hardwood floor in the hotel lobby. She was thankful for work that kept her hands and mind occupied, despite the fact that her back ached and her hands were rubbed raw from the vibration of the sander. Still, anything was better than letting her mind wander to Dylan.

Pushing the goggles she wore onto the top of her head, she stepped back and admired the bare oak planks. There was a fine layer of sawdust on everything, including herself. Especially herself, she decided, looking down at her jeans and what had been a pink blouse.

"Nice job."

Startled, she turned abruptly at the sound of Dylan's voice. He stood in the doorway behind her, arms folded, scanning her work with a critical eye.

Except for meals, she'd seen very little of him for the past four days. He'd surprised her two days ago by installing an electric stove he'd bought at a secondhand store in Cactus

Flat. She'd complained it disrupted the antiquity of the kitchen. He told her she could bury it if she wanted after he left, but until he was gone, the stove stayed. Needless to say, the quality of the food had improved considerably.

"Thanks." She accepted his compliment, knowing how rare words of praise were from Dylan. The man was a perfectionist, she'd realized after watching him work, and expected the same from the men who worked for him. But the church was slowly taking shape, and its original beauty returning.

"Have the men gone home already?" she asked.

He nodded. "I let them go a little early. They hustled this week and we're already ahead of schedule."

Jessica watched Dylan comb his hair away from his face with his hands. *It's not fair,* she thought. After a hard day's work, with dirt on his clothes and sweat on his face and arms, he still looked good. She looked like a wood-shop cat.

She brushed some of the sawdust from her arms and tugged the goggles from her head. "Dinner's going to be a little late tonight. The chicken wasn't thawed."

"I'm sorry, Jessica. I forgot to tell you I won't be here tonight. I'm going into town."

She felt like an idiot when disappointment shot through her. Of course he wouldn't be here tonight. It was Friday. He'd go into town with the other guys and do what single men did on Friday night, which usually included beer and female company. Cactus Flat might be a small town, but there were plenty of women who'd be happy to keep a man like Dylan company. He probably wouldn't come back all weekend.

But whatever Dylan did with his leisure time was certainly his business, she told herself. She just prayed she wouldn't have to hear about it from one of the town gossips.

"No problem." She gave a shrug and shook sawdust from her hair. "It won't go to waste." *Not if I have to eat the whole damn thing myself.*

"You sure?" he asked.

"Of course." She'd made a chocolate cake earlier, too, to celebrate the first week of construction. She decided to eat that by herself, as well.

"Look, I can go to town a little later. It's really not—"

"Dylan, for heaven's sake, don't think about it. Go to town."

His jaw flexed. "All right. You need anything while I'm there?"

She shook her head, then tucked her hair behind her ears. "I'm going in tomorrow to do some Christmas shopping."

He frowned, then stepped in front of her. "Let me see your hands."

"What?"

"Your hands." He reached out and took her wrists, then pulled her toward him. His frown deepened as he stared at her red palms. "Why weren't you wearing gloves?"

It was only a touch, not even an intimate one, but still her heart was hammering so loud she thought for sure Dylan would hear. "I'm fine," she said tightly, and tried to pull away. He held firm.

"You need to put something on this to ease the burning," he said, his voice strangely rough.

She'd have to put something on her entire body, Jessica thought. She felt hot all over, inside and out, and she doubted that anything other than the man holding her could ever ease that.

His thumbs moved gently over her wrists, then her palms. The heat built until she felt limp. Self-preservation had her pulling away. "I'll take care of it."

He stared at her for what felt like hours, though it was only a few seconds. "See that you do."

He moved past her, up the stairs and into his room. She closed her eyes and let out a long breath. *Forget the chicken,* she thought. She was heading straight for the chocolate cake.

A three-quarter moon hung low in the sky by the time Dylan cut the engine on his bike and cruised quietly into Makeshift. It was barely past nine, hardly what a bachelor would consider late, but he'd been anxious to get back for two hours.

Hell, he'd been anxious to get back before he'd even left.

He wouldn't have gone at all if he hadn't promised to meet Jared and Jake. They all knew it was risky trying to talk with Jessica around, so they'd arranged a coincidental we-just-ran-into-each-other meeting at the Rock Slide Bar. Dylan had been relieved when both Jake and Jared had left early, but when one of the crew spotted him in the smoke-filled bar he'd been forced into hanging out for a while longer.

Removing his helmet, he looked up at the hotel and saw that the only light came from her room. He frowned. Jessica rarely went to her room this early. In fact, she was usually up half the night. He often heard her talking to Hannibal or listening to music on the radio. Too often he'd found himself staring mindlessly at the set of blueprints he'd been working on, wondering what she was doing, or even worse, what she was wearing. He'd lost count of the pencil tips he'd broken during those thoughts.

With a long sigh, he raked his fingers through his hair and went into the quiet hotel. He knew it was for the best that she'd retreated. During the day it was easy to avoid her, especially with all the crew around.

It was the nights that preyed on him, made him think about things he shouldn't think about, want things he shouldn't want. Seeing Jake and Jared tonight was a fresh reminder that she was out-of-bounds, and for that, he was glad he'd gone to town. He definitely needed a memory jolt when it came to Jessica and why he was here.

He made his way silently through the darkness into the kitchen. He hadn't eaten in town. After thinking about the dinner Jessica said she was preparing, the greasy fries and hot dogs at the bar hadn't appealed to him. *I'm getting soft,* he decided, but started for the refrigerator, anyway, hoping there might be leftovers, then froze when something cold and wet brushed his hand.

Hannibal.

Laughing at himself, Dylan bent down to pet the dog. "How you doing, boy?" Dylan ruffled the animal's fur. "Jessica asleep already?"

That was when he heard the voices.

He stopped, listening carefully. A man's voice. And a woman's. Talking softly. Not loud enough to hear the words, but the tone and inflection were definitely amorous.

He squinted into the darkness, straining to make out what was being said and where it was coming from. Upstairs, he decided, and slowly moved out of the kitchen toward the stairs. Hannibal padded alongside him, unconcerned, though Dylan was certain the dog heard the voices, as well.

Dylan stood at the base of the stairs. He heard the soft sound of a feminine laugh.

No wonder she'd practically pushed him out the door earlier this evening. She'd been expecting someone. There was a man up there now. Were they in bed? A slow unreasonable fury began to build in him. Whoever it was, it obviously was someone Hannibal knew, or he wouldn't have left Jessica alone.

Fists clenched, Dylan moved up the stairs. He should have stayed in town, he told himself. There'd been a cute blonde who'd tried repeatedly to catch his eye. And a curvy redhead who'd sidled up next to him when he'd been talking to Jared. He could have had a few laughs and relieved a little stress with either one of those ladies.

But much to his irritation, every time he'd looked at the blonde or redhead, all he saw was a blue-eyed brunette covered with sawdust wearing plastic goggles on her head.

He resisted the temptation to stomp up the stairs and, instead, moved quietly into his room. He heard music now. Classical. Soft and low, with violins. Vivaldi, he thought. It came from Jessica's room.

Dammit! Who was in there with her?

He paced, and the sudden absence of voices had him grinding his teeth. Hannibal sat in the middle of the floor and watched him stride back and forth.

Dylan thought about leaving. Just getting on his bike and going back to town. It was certainly none of his business if Jessica had company. Nor was it any of his business what they were doing.

The silence made his stomach knot. He did have an obligation to make sure she was all right, he reasoned. That's why he was here, after all, whether she knew it or not.

He moved into the bathroom that separated their rooms. Jessica's door to the bathroom was ajar, and a faint light spilled over the wood floor. *Get the hell out of here,* he argued with himself.

His fingers were stiff as he slowly opened Jessica's door wider and looked into the room.

She sat on the edge of the bed, one long bare leg stretched out across the quilt, the other bare leg bent at the knee. Her head was bowed as she leaned forward, her hair a curtain across her face. She had a small bottle in her hand and was dabbing at her toenails.

Confused, Dylan quickly scanned the room. Unless the guy had hidden under the bed, she was alone.

He looked back at her and his heart stopped.

She wore silk. An ivory chemise that shimmered in the pale glow of the oil lamp. Mesmerized, he watched her slender fingers carefully brush red polish over each toenail. He knew he should turn away, but it was beyond his ability.

His gaze moved over her long legs. Her skin looked like porcelain, and he curled his fingers at the thought of running his hand up the curve of her hip and over her breasts.

He stood in the middle of a tug-of-war, the captivating sight of Jessica pulling him in one direction, reason and decency pulling him in the other. A woman had never made him feel like this before. A need rose in him so intense, so desperate, he no longer felt in control.

Her head tilted, and he could see her face now. She'd captured her bottom lip between her teeth. He nearly groaned at the seductive gesture. He had to get out of here. Now.

That was when she glanced up at him.

Her eyes widened, and her lips parted as she stared back at him. "Dylan?" Her voice was no more than a strained whisper.

Dammit. Dammit. He felt like a Peeping Tom. Hell, he *was* a Peeping Tom.

"I'm sorry," he said hoarsely, surprised he was able to speak at all. "I heard voices."

She capped the bottle in her hand and set it on the nightstand. With one fluid movement she swung her legs off the bed and reached for a floral robe behind her.

"A man and woman?"

Her breasts pressed against her chemise as she pulled the robe on, and the outline of her nipples against the thin silk made his throat as dry as the pile of sawdust on the hotel-lobby floor. Rather than croak a reply, he simply nodded.

"Meggie and Lucas," she said, cinching the belt of her robe. "They spend a lot of time here at the hotel, usually in the room at the end of the hall."

Her statement brought him slowly out of the fog he'd felt captured in. She was talking about her ghosts. Here, in the hotel. If her expression hadn't been so serious, he might have laughed. She reached over and flipped off the radio beside her bed when a commercial came on. He realized it was the radio he'd heard before, but if Jessica wanted to believe it was ghosts, he wouldn't argue.

He decided that even if Jessica was a bit strange, she was still beautiful. The soft light framed her slender form on the bed, and he felt an overwhelming need to touch her, to feel her under him as he laid her back on that bed and covered her body with his.

He looked around the room again, searching the corners. "I thought you had someone up here with you."

"In my bedroom?"

He moved into the room, though he only dared a step. "I heard a man's voice."

She raised an eyebrow. "So you assumed I had a man in my bed."

"I just wanted to make sure you're all right, that's all." He knew he had no business questioning her on her private life, but somehow that thought didn't stop him. She met his steady gaze, and his body flooded with heat. He was treading on thin ice here, and if he wasn't careful, he'd fall through. It took every ounce of concentration to keep from staring at her legs or thinking about what she was wearing under that robe.

It took every ounce of Jessica's concentration to keep from shaking like a leaf. Dylan had startled her when she'd looked up and found him watching her, but the look in his eyes had been far more disturbing than his unexpected appearance. For a moment the look had been wild, like a predator's. Then he'd glanced away, and when he looked back his expression was controlled again, unreadable. Still, her heart raced, and she struggled desperately for composure.

"I'm fine, Dylan," she said quietly. "Other than the fact you just scared me half to death. I didn't expect you back from town until tomorrow."

He frowned. "Why?"

"You *are* single."

"Oh." He looked at her. "I guess we both assume a lot about each other, Jessica. I'll let you know when I'm staying in town."

"All right." She nodded. "And I'll let you know when I have company."

A muscle twitched in Dylan's jaw. "You do that."

"And if you decide to bring a *guest* back here," she said, "just warn me."

It was all Dylan could do not to show Jessica exactly what he did with a *guest* in his bedroom. What did she think? That they were roommates, for God's sake?

But then, what else were they? There was certainly nothing between them. There couldn't be. So why was he suddenly feeling as if he wanted to smash a wall because she might want some male companionship? She was a grown woman. A gorgeous, seductive grown woman.

It had definitely been a mistake coming in here. Not his first where Jessica was concerned, but he was determined it was going to be his last.

"I'll do that," he said tightly. "Good night."

"Night."

He closed the door behind him. When he finally went to bed sometime in the early morning, he was still hungry. But this time, it had nothing to do with food.

Dylan sat at the kitchen table working on the final touches of the blueprints while he ate the sandwich Jessica had left in the refrigerator for him before she'd left for town earlier. Except for the chicken dinner, he'd shared every meal with her since he'd moved here, and as much as he hated to admit it, he missed her company.

The crew had already gone back to work, and Dylan could hear hammering and the buzz of saws. They'd moved into the second week of construction, and the roof, inner walls and floors of the church were already finished. They still needed to paint inside and out, plus hang the windows and finish the pews. Jessica was planning a Christmas gathering with her family there, and Dylan didn't want to disappoint her.

Even he had begun to feel the excitement of the coming holiday. He'd never really had a Christmas growing up—at least, not like other kids. His parents had divorced when he was six, and both had avidly pursued the fine art of remarriage several times each, leaving Dylan either with the headmaster at Kingsley Academy in Maine or with his mother's housekeeper at her summer home in Florida.

He'd escaped that life when he was eighteen, went straight to work for a construction company in Colorado, put himself through university, then eventually went overseas with an American construction company that specialized in oil wells.

"Hannibal!" Dylan turned at the sound of Jessica's voice. "Hold on, will you?"

She moved haltingly into the kitchen, juggling three bags of groceries, trying not to step on Hannibal, who circled her legs excitedly.

"Just wait a minute," she said with exasperation.

Dylan rose and took two bags from her. When their hands brushed, he felt a jolt of electricity, then quickly turned away and set the bags on the counter.

"Thanks." She set her bag next to the others and pulled out a box of dog biscuits. Hannibal barked as she opened them, then sat, tail wagging. She opened the back door and tossed one outside. The dog bounded out after it.

"Want one?" she asked Dylan, holding up another biscuit.

He lifted a brow. "You trying to tell me something?"

She smiled slowly. "Whatever would that be?"

Her gaze fell on the kitchen table then, and she looked back at him, her eyes wide. "Are those the blueprints?"

He nodded.

She moved beside the table and stared at the drawings. "They're wonderful," she said breathlessly.

Her pleasure brought a strange pressure to his chest. "There're still details to add," he said. "But it's clear enough for anyone with even a little experience to read."

"You mean—" her gaze met his "—when you're not here."

He'd made it clear from the beginning he only wanted temporary work. The project would carry on fine without him. She would carry on fine without him. So why was he suddenly feeling so damn guilty? "Look, Jessica, you'll be able to—"

"Oh, hello there. Am I interrupting?"

Dylan turned sharply. It was Myrna. Dressed in a white jumpsuit, she stood in the doorway, a bright red smile plastered on her face. Managing to contain the swear word on the tip of his tongue, Dylan moved away from Jessica.

The click of Myrna's red high heels echoed as she moved across the hardwood floor toward them. "Jessica, dear, where have you been keeping yourself?"

As far away from you as possible, Jessica thought as she stood and faced her stepmother. "I've been busy here."

"You're too young to be working so hard," Myrna said, then looked at Dylan. "Hello, Mr. Grant."

He nodded. "Mrs. Stone."

"Daddy and I noticed you have some men working on the church. I must admit, dear, we *are* surprised."

"And why is that?"

"It must be very costly replacing a building so badly damaged. But then, most of this town *is* quite deteriorated."

Here it comes, Jessica thought. She wasn't in the mood for this. Not now.

Without so much as batting one heavily mascaraed eyelash, Myrna started in. "Jessica—" she waved a hand impatiently "—it's going to cost a fortune to rebuild this town.

It should have been leveled fifty years ago. When are you going to wake up from this fantasy world of yours and face reality?"

Jessica sighed. "And I suppose you think that building stables out here and breeding racehorses is reality?"

Myrna lifted her chin. "It's a sound investment. Daddy thinks so, too."

"You hate horses, Myrna. How are you going to breed and train them?"

"I'll hire people to do that, of course. Stone Creek Stables, I'm going to call it. We'll be famous."

Jessica heard Dylan's grunt of laughter, but ignored it. "I'll not selling Makeshift, Myrna. Not one acre, not one inch. You'll have to find something else to be famous for somewhere else."

"Jessica, living in these dilapidated old buildings is dangerous. How can you even sleep?"

Sleep was definitely becoming a problem, Jessica thought, but it had nothing to do with old buildings and everything to do with Dylan.

"Myrna, are you pestering Jessica again?"

Myrna frowned as her father entered the kitchen. "I'm not pestering anyone. Jessica's just too stubborn, that's all."

"Stone determination," Carlton said with admiration. "Your late husband taught his children well. Too bad that man never went into business with me. We would have made a fortune. Good afternoon, Jessica. Mr. Grant."

Dylan nodded to the other man. "Dylan, please."

Jessica watched as the two men shook hands. She noticed that Carlton wasn't as pale as he'd been at the party for Jared, and he moved less stiffly today. He was dressed casually, in gray slacks and a polo shirt, and looked remarkably younger. She hoped that meant there'd been an improvement in his condition.

"You've done a fine job here, young man," Carlton said to Dylan. "I never would have thought that church was salvageable."

"It looked worse than it was," Dylan said. "But I give all the credit to my crew. They're hardworking dependable men."

Carlton shook his head. "Don't be modest, my boy. It's good leadership that makes a project succeed. Good leadership and careful planning. I could use a man like you in one of my companies."

Dylan glanced up at the sound of shouting from outside. Frowning, he went through the lobby and into the street. Jessica followed, trailed by Myrna and Carlton. The crew hurried up the street from the church. Max, the supervising carpenter, led the pack.

"Sorry, boss," Max said, stopping in front of Dylan. His voice shook. "But you're going to have to find a new crew."

"A new crew!" Dylan looked at each man. Their faces were white, their eyes wide. "What are you talking about?"

"It's one thing to hear stories. I mean, who believes it?" Sweat dripped from Max's forehead. "But when it's right in your face, Lordy, it's something different."

"Max, what the hell are you talking about?"

"Ghosts, boss. That's what we're talking about. In the church. We're outta here."

Six
***

"**I** can't believe Lucas or Meggie would object to the rebuilding." Jessica paced the length of the kitchen. After a frenzied afternoon, everyone else, including Myrna and Carlton, had finally left. "Especially the church."

Dylan leaned against the counter, arms folded, face set tight. "According to Max, they not only objected, they picked up a hammer and threw it right at him."

Jessica dragged her hands through her hair as she continued to pace. "It can't be. Meggie and Lucas would never hurt anyone—" she hesitated "—unless there was a reason of course."

Dylan frowned. "The men aren't convinced."

Jessica groaned. "So he actually saw Meggie? Really saw her?"

"He believes he saw something. And so did the other men who were in the church. They also heard voices, a man and a woman arguing."

Jessica shook her head. "Meggie and Lucas never argue."

"Yeah, well, I've seen the strongest relationship dissolve when it comes to remodeling."

Jessica threw her hands. "I've just lost my work crew and you're making jokes. I can't believe this."

He took hold of her shoulders, forcing her to look at him. "Have you considered the possibility that someone staged this?"

She frowned. "What are you talking about?"

"If no one will work here, you can't build your town, right?"

She didn't like what he was getting at. "Of course not."

"And didn't you tell me that a review board comes here in January to assess your progress and determine if they'll grant you a license?"

She nodded.

"And what happens if you don't get your license?"

She didn't want to think about it. She couldn't. "Why would anyone do that to me?"

"Myrna wants this land. Someone else might, too. Or maybe someone doesn't want you to build a youth center here. You tell me."

It was a strong possibility, Jessica knew that. Especially after what Jared and Jake had gone through the past few months with someone sabotaging their land. Sam and Myrna had both wanted to buy Makeshift, but Sam had never pestered her about it. And Myrna. Well, Myrna was just Myrna. Jessica hadn't believed before that her stepmother had anything to do with the problems Jake and Jared had, and she didn't believe she had anything to do with this, either.

She sighed heavily. But whether it was Meggie and Lucas or whether it was someone else, the effect was the same. If no one would work here, she'd fall behind schedule. She couldn't let that happen.

She met Dylan's steady gaze. "We have to find another crew, Dylan. We have to."

He moved his hands up her shoulders to her neck. His fingers were warm on her skin, and she wanted desperately to lean into him.

"I'll have to bring in men from farther away," he said, and his voice sounded thick. "It's going to take some time."

He let his hands fall away, then looked at her for a long moment and left. Her skin still burned where he'd touched her. With a sigh, Jessica sank back against the counter. Time was something she did not have in abundance.

She looked at the blueprints still lying on the table. Makeshift was her town. The kids needed it. *She* needed it.

She *was* going to build it.

She just had to figure out how.

"Don't cry, Meggie," Lucas said softly. "Please don't cry."

Meggie sat in the front church pew, her face buried in her hands. "Oh, Lucas, Jessica must be so angry with me."

"She's not angry. She may not understand, but she knows we'd never do anything to hurt her."

Lucas sat beside Meggie. It was starting to get dark, and soft evening light streamed in through the tall narrow windows of the church. Meggie looked like an angel, he thought. A true angel. She'd been crying since the men had run off, and it broke his heart to see her so miserable.

"And why did that man say we were arguing?" she said between sobs. "We were simply discussing whether they'd properly placed the altar when he sneaked up on us."

Lucas smiled. "I'm afraid he was right, Meggie, dear. We were arguing."

She sniffed indignantly. "Well, it might not matter to you, but the altar does belong closer to the front row. Mrs. Wimple wouldn't be able to hear if the altar was set back too far."

He didn't have the heart to remind her Mrs. Wimple was gone, as was everyone else.

"And I most certainly did not throw a hammer at him," *she said sharply. "I was simply moving it before it fell on that piece of glass he was replacing."*

"I know."

She looked up at him, and the light reflected off the tears in her eyes. "How did this happen, Lucas? How could that man have seen me? No one has ever seen either of us. Well, except for Hannibal."

Lucas didn't understand it, either. They'd always needed to be careful about their voices, but no one had ever seen them. Something was happening here. He felt . . . stronger. And Meggie was glowing brighter. Was it because of the church? Was it possible that, if the church was rebuilt, he and Meggie might be able to move on, as they should have so long ago?

Lucas had no idea. But he prayed Jessica and Dylan would soon have that answer for him.

Dylan had been in Jessica's bedroom all morning using her phone. He'd made a dozen calls to every contact he had within a six-hundred-mile radius, but he was batting zero. There were some possibilities in three weeks, but no one wanted to start a new job during the holidays.

He paced, wondering if he should expand his radius, then gave up that idea. He could call to South America and it wouldn't matter. The chance of finding a replacement crew before the New Year was somewhere between almost none and none.

He sighed heavily and sat on the edge of Jessica's bed. She'd driven into town earlier, determined to place an ad in the local paper. But he'd seen what she'd come up with the first time she used that technique, and he held little hope that this time would be any different.

Her mattress was soft, he realized. Like she was. The scent of jasmine drifted from her pillow. His sleep had become practically nonexistent as he thought of her each night in here, dressed in silk and lace. He could still vividly see her long bare arms and legs, her smooth thighs and round breasts. He even thought of those damn red toes of hers.

Every time she took a bath or shower, he made sure he had something to do elsewhere. The sound of the water conjured up images that nearly drove him mad.

The persistent honk of a car horn had him jumping up guiltily. He looked out the window and saw Jessica pulling up in front of the hotel. Several young men climbed out of the bed of her truck. Another truck and a small sedan pulled alongside.

What the hell was she up to? he wondered, and went down to meet her on the hotel steps. Her companions, five of them, fell in behind.

"Dylan. I want you to meet some friends of mine." Jessica smiled brightly and turned to her entourage.

"This is Tony—" a pencil-thin redhead smiled "—Peter—" a dark-haired, dark-skinned kid nodded "—Larry—" a short-haired, diamond-stud-in-the-ear blonde raised his hand "—Josh—" a barrel-chested kid with curly brown hair stuck out his hand "—and Dean."

The last kid was tall and lanky with piercing gray eyes and black hair. He stood back from the rest, leaning against Jessica's truck, his arms folded.

Impatience rippled through Dylan. Here he was, facing total shutdown of the project, and Jessica was bringing company to visit. He didn't have time for this.

"You'll have to excuse me," he said tightly, forcing his irritation down, "but I've got more phone calls to make. I'm trying to find us a crew."

He started to turn away, but Jessica took hold of his arm and pulled him back. "That's what I'm trying to tell you. This *is* your crew."

He stared at her blankly. "What did you say?"

"This is your new crew. Plus four more tomorrow."

He looked at the kids again, then back at Jessica. His first impulse was to say she must be kidding, but he knew she wasn't. She was dead serious. "I don't think you understand, Jessica. I need qualified men, *experienced* men."

Dylan felt the bristling among the group, especially Dean, who narrowed his eyes and pushed away from the truck.

"They *are* experienced, Dylan. Each of them has worked with their fathers or for someone else in the building trades. Especially Dean. He's been framing houses for a local builder for two years."

Dylan looked at the youth, who glared back.

Taking hold of Jessica's arm, Dylan pulled her inside the hotel. "Are you out of your mind? We aren't building a tree house here. This is hard work, long hours. These are kids. Kids who should be in school, I might add."

Frowning, Jessica put a finger to her lips. "They all have vacation until after the first of the year, plus several of them are on home study. And they want to work. They just need someone to give them a chance." She leaned close, her expression fervent. "Everyone deserves at least one chance, Dylan. Don't you believe that?"

He did, dammit. Dylan had barely turned eighteen when Tom Quincy hired him on blind faith and taught him how to swing a hammer. God only knew where he'd have ended up if the man hadn't given him a chance. He swore silently.

"This isn't one chance, Jessica. It's *nine.* I'll have to hold hands with every one of them. Time and mistakes are both money. Can you afford that?"

She lifted her gaze to his. "Dylan, don't you understand? That's what Makeshift is all about. We can't afford *not* to. It's why I'm here, why I'm doing this. Please, just give it a try." She leaned closer still and placed her hands on his arms. "Please."

He felt her body tense against his, and her whispered plea circled him like a net. He was caught. She could have asked him to build a skyscraper with paper clips and he would have done it.

And at this point he didn't have any better ideas, either.

He looked up at the ceiling and sighed. "I'm going to regret this."

She laughed, then reached up and kissed his cheek. "You won't. I promise."

When she went out to tell the kids, he shook his head and let out a long slow breath. The scent of her lingered, and his cheek felt warm where her lips had been.

She was wrong, he thought. He already did regret it.

"I think I'm going to be sick." Annie closed her eyes and sank onto the chair in front of the dressing table. Strains of Beethoven floated in from the church organ outside, and the scent of roses filled the air.

"No, you're not." Jessica handed Annie a soda cracker. "You're too beautiful to be sick."

"You'll be fine," Savannah said, hooking the clasp of Annie's pearl necklace. "And Jessica's right. You're the most beautiful bride I've ever seen."

Annie shook her head. "I saw your wedding pictures. *You* were."

Because the conversation distracted Annie, Jessica didn't interrupt as she and Savannah disputed who was the more beautiful bride. They were both beautiful of course. Breathtakingly so.

Emma sat on the sofa, kicking her feet as she fidgeted with the flowers in her basket. "How much longer?" she asked.

Jessica stuck her head out the door. Jared and Jake stood at the front of the church by a huge arrangement of red and white flowers. Jared glanced nervously at his watch. She scanned the crowded pews, then her heart tripped as one figure sat taller than the rest.

Dylan?

"Annie," she said, her pulse racing as she turned back to her soon-to-be sister-in-law, "did you invite Dylan?"

"Jared did." Annie clipped on a pearl-drop earring. "I guess he ran into him last night in town at his bachelor party and they had a few beers."

Jared invited *Dylan?* Jessica couldn't believe it. Jared barely spoke to Dylan, and now he'd invited him to his wedding? And where did he get that suit he had on? He looked absolutely devastating.

"I saw Dylan this morning before Savannah picked me up," Jessica said thoughtfully. "He never mentioned he was coming."

"Maybe he decided at the last minute." Savannah adjusted Annie's veil. "And since it's just we girls, you want to tell us what's going on with you two?"

Jessica felt her cheeks warm. "Well, we just hired a few of the kids from my teen group in town, and they've been terrific. Even Dean Johnson, one of the most reluctant kids in the group, has—"

"That's not what we mean, Jessie, and you know it." Savannah nudged Annie. "She's almost as red as her dress, Annie. Something's up."

Jessica forced herself to stop staring at Dylan and closed the door, pretending sudden interest in straightening the hair she'd swept up on her head. "Nothing at all is up. We work together, that's all."

"She's in the denial stage," Annie said knowingly. Savannah nodded with a sigh.

Jessica pressed her lips together. "There's nothing to deny."

"Stubborn. Just like her brothers." Savannah picked up a tube of lipstick and swept the rose color over her lips.

"Look me in the eye, Jess," she said, "and tell me the man's not gorgeous."

"I also happen to know from a reliable source that she likes, uh, attractive posteriors, too." Annie glanced at Emma, who was humming and counting rose petals. "I've also noticed that she's noticed the said subject, if you know what I mean."

Jessica ground her teeth. She'd mentioned to Annie a long time ago that she was particular to that part of a man's anatomy. She certainly regretted it now. "Okay. So he's not hard to look at, especially from behind. That means nothing. He's not my type."

"Girl," Savannah drawled in her heaviest Georgia accent, "that man is *every* woman's type. And the way he looks at you isn't exactly with indifference. I'd throw those potatoes in a pot and bring them to a boil if I were you."

A knock at the door startled them. Eyes wide, Annie jumped up. Her skin glowed, and her eyes shined brightly.

"You look beautiful," Jessica whispered to Annie, then squeezed both women's hands. "I couldn't have found better sisters-in-law."

Emma joined them and they all hugged, then Annie picked up her bouquet and sucked in a deep breath. "Let's do it."

The church was crowded with friends and family for the bride and groom. Jessica's heart hammered as she followed Savannah down the aisle, and when her gaze met Dylan's, she nearly stumbled. No man had ever looked at her the way he was. As if she were the only woman in the room. The only woman in the world.

As if he wanted her. *Really* wanted her.

She looked quickly away. But he didn't want her. He'd made that perfectly clear.

Dylan forgot to breathe as he watched Jessica walk down the aisle. His pulse pounded in his temple as she passed him, and the brief glance she sent him made his heart lurch. He tried to watch the ceremony, tried to listen to the minister, but all he saw, all he thought about, was Jessica.

She was dressed in red. A form-fitting knee-length number that could make a man forget his own name. She'd piled that thick shiny hair of hers on top of her head somehow, and curls cascaded down her long neck. His palms itched every time he looked at that neck, and his gut tightened painfully every time he looked at her spectacular legs.

He watched her cry when Jared kissed Annie, then laugh when the bride and groom ran through a shower of confetti outside the church. He watched her smile for pictures and for the toasts, watched her sip champagne, and later, after the band played the bridal waltz, he did what he'd wanted to do from the first moment he'd watched her walk down that aisle: he pulled her into his arms and out onto the dance floor.

It was a slow dance. He wouldn't have bothered with anything else. He'd deprived himself of enough when it came to Jessica. He'd have this dance, just one, and be done with it.

"Nice wedding," he murmured, though he really didn't feel like talking. She was stiff in his arms, but soft and warm. He breathed in the scent of her, pulling it into his lungs and holding it.

"Yes."

Her formal tone frustrated him, but he knew she wasn't unaffected by their closeness. He felt her body tremble, and when his fingers brushed her wrist, the rapid pulse of her heart betrayed her. Desire swam through him like a living breathing creature, and he struggled to control the beast. *One dance,* he told himself. He could manage one dance.

Jessica felt light-headed, though she'd only had one glass of champagne. Every nerve focused on the man holding her. His cheek brushed hers. His hand rested on the small of her back. She felt the heat of his body, smelled his after-shave. The black suit emphasized his broad chest and muscular shoulders, and the combination of smooth sophistication and rugged masculinity left her breathless.

"Jared and Annie look happy." Dylan glanced over at the bride and groom.

Jessica smiled, relieved to have her attention pulled elsewhere. "They had a tough time getting together. Jared felt guilty after our brother's death, and he didn't think he deserved happiness. That's why he ran off to South America for almost four years."

"It's easy to get lost in Venezuela," Dylan said quietly.

She looked at him. "I never mentioned Venezuela."

He pulled her a little closer. "Didn't you? I guess Jared must have said something last night."

His warm breath fanned her neck and she couldn't stop the ripple of need that coursed through her.

"I admit I'm surprised that Jared invited you today," she said, inching away. "But I'm also glad he's not so hostile anymore."

"No doubt that getting married put him in an agreeable mood."

"Maybe you should try it, then." Jessica smiled as Digger danced by with Annie's mother. "Just to improve your disposition."

"I tried it. Had the opposite effect, I'm afraid."

Jessica faltered. He'd said the words without the slightest hint of emotion. As if he was simply stating a cold fact. "So one lost race puts you out of the running, huh? I never took you for a quitter, Dylan."

She forced her tone to be light and her manner aloof, when she was anything but. Dylan loosened his hold on her, and the heat that had nearly exploded between them cooled.

He gazed down at her, his dark eyes intense. "The only thing I quit is making mistakes."

Neither one of them had realized the slow dance had ended. The band struck up a fast swing number, and before Dylan could blink, Jessica was yanked from his arms by Jared's foreman, Hugh Slater.

Her gaze stayed on Dylan's as she danced with the other man. He watched her, and he ached to hold her against him again. But he'd had his dance, he thought as he turned away. He'd have to be satisfied with that.

He made his way to the bar, where he found Jake nursing a beer. His tie and cummerbund had been loosened long ago, and his black Stetson was tipped precariously on his head. He slapped Dylan on the back and motioned for the bartender to bring a beer. Jared joined them a moment later, and the three men leaned back against the bar.

Jake gestured to the dance floor. "My little sister's really something, isn't she?"

Even before he swung his glance around, Dylan knew it was a mistake. If he couldn't hold her in his arms, he sure as hell didn't want to watch any other man hold her.

She was still dancing with Slater, not a slow dance, more like a hard-rock number, which she moved sensuously to. Dylan took in her swaying curves and high-heeled legs and felt as if he'd been poleaxed. Sweat broke out on his forehead when she dipped forward.

Dylan took a long hard pull on his beer. "Yeah. She's something all right."

"How's that crew of hers working out?" Jared asked.

Dylan turned back around. "So far pretty good. They're green, but eager to work. They even showed up this morning. I haven't had a crew that wanted to work on Saturday in years."

"Have they seen anything unusual?" Jake asked.

He shook his head. "I still can't find any logical reason why the old crew quit. I don't buy the ghost story, but I'm keeping a close eye on things."

"I don't know what we would've done without you, pal. Jake and I definitely owe you one." Jared grinned over at Dylan. "Jessica giving you trouble?"

Trouble? Dylan nearly laughed. She was trouble with a capital *T*. But not the kind that Jared meant. "No, but if she asks, you mentioned Venezuela to me in town Friday night."

Jared hadn't time to answer before his new bride stood in front of him, and Savannah in front of Jake. A slow romantic song filled the air. Jake and Jared both grinned and pushed away from the bar.

"Be right back, Dylan. The Stone men never miss an opportunity to hold a beautiful woman in their arms."

Dylan looked at Jessica, who was dancing with Sam now. The Stone women didn't miss an opportunity with a man, either, he thought irritably. "I'll be heading out in a minute. Thanks for inviting me." He shook Jared's hand, then Jake's, and smiled at Savannah and Annie. "I'd take Jessica home, but I've got my bike."

"Don't worry," Savannah said over her shoulder as she tugged Jake onto the dance floor. "Sam's taking her home. She'll be in good hands."

In good hands. Sam's hands. That image had Dylan tightening his hold around the bottle in his hand. He glanced back at the dance floor, gritting his teeth at the sight of Jessica's arms looped around Sam's neck. He began to swear under his breath, then quickly caught himself as he realized Emma stood staring at him.

He forced a smile. "Hi."

"Hi." She kept staring intently, her eyes narrowed. She moved to the side of him and looked behind him.

"Something wrong?" he asked.

She shook her head slowly. "Jessica told Savannah and Annie you aren't hard to look at. I don't think so, either."

Dylan lifted a brow. "Thanks. She say anything else?"

"She said you look good from behind, too, but I like you better from the front."

Dylan struggled to hold back the laugh in his throat. "Thanks again. I think you look pretty good, too."

"Thanks."

From the mouths of babes, Dylan thought with a chuckle as Emma skipped off. His chuckle faded quickly, though, as he glanced back at Jessica. Sam held her closer still, and she didn't seem to mind a bit. She smiled up at him, whispering something into his ear. Sam laughed.

Dylan's insides knotted and he slammed his beer down. He'd had enough beer and enough Jessica. He'd wanted to be here for Jared, but he'd never been good at parties, especially weddings. He needed a long ride on his bike in the fresh air to cool his blood, anyway.

But almost two hours later, after he'd made it back to Makeshift, his blood hadn't cooled. In fact, when he realized that Jessica still wasn't home, his temperature moved steadily upward, degree by degree, with each passing minute.

He sat at the foot of the stairs with Hannibal and stared at the antique grandfather clock Jessica had placed in the lobby. It ticked loudly. What if they'd had an accident? Sam could have drunk too much. Jessica could be lying in a ditch somewhere, hurt.

Twelve o'clock bonged with a deafening echo.

He stood, pacing the foyer, imagining other scenarios and reasons she might be late.

But he kept coming back to the same one: Jessica, with Sam, in his bed.

The clock chimed the quarter, then half hour. Then one o'clock.

He'd go look for her, dammit. If she was with Sam, then fine, but at least he'd know. Then he could forget about it. About her.

Yeah. Right.

He was heading for the front door when he heard a truck drive up. He looked out. Sam's truck. Hannibal lifted his head, listening to the string of curses Dylan shot out when Jessica didn't come in right away. He was seriously considering sending the dog out for her when the hotel door opened.

She came in quietly, shoes in her hand, and slowly closed the door behind her. She started to tiptoe across the lobby when she suddenly caught sight of Dylan sitting at the foot of the stairs. Startled, she looked at him. Several curls had come loose from the knot on top of her head, and her cheeks were flushed.

"It's after one in the morning." Dylan grabbed hold of the banister and stood. "Party went kind of late."

"And you left kind of early," she said, her gaze holding his. "Without saying goodbye, I might add."

"Yeah, well, you were busy with Sam at the time."

"I wasn't that busy."

He watched the sway of her hips as she moved slowly toward him. "Don't you think you should have let me know you're all right?"

"Why?" she asked.

Did she have to look so damn seductive? he wondered. Was she doing this to him on purpose? "You could've been in an accident."

"Do I look like I was in an accident?" Her voice was almost a purr as she held out her arms.

He let his gaze skim over her curves in the snug red dress. His groin tightened painfully. She didn't look as if she'd been in an accident, but she certainly might cause one. "So where were you?"

She shook her head slowly and sighed. "Good night, Dylan. I'm going to bed."

He caught her arm when she started to move past him. "I was worried about you."

Her eyes glittered like blue ice. "I already have two brothers who worry enough, thank you. I don't need, or want, another one."

He held her still when she tried to yank her arm away. "Of all the things I want, Jessica," he said roughly, "being your brother is not one of them."

Her eyes turned a deep blue as she searched his face. "What is it you want, Dylan?" she asked softly. "What?"

"This."

He couldn't pretend any longer. He couldn't deny it. It was suddenly all too much, wanting her as he did, needing to feel her body against his.

With an oath, he dragged her against him and covered her mouth with his.

Seven

The force of his mouth caught Jessica completely off guard. His kiss was hungry and hard, long and deep. She clung to him, at first to steady herself, then mindlessly, helplessly, with a need that had been denied for too long. She knew it was crazy, knew she would surely regret this, but his lips sought hers with a desperation that left her weak.

She moaned into his mouth, meeting the thrust of his tongue with her own. He shuddered, tightening his hold on her, dragging her closer, molding her body intimately to his. Her shoes clattered to the floor.

He slanted his lips against hers again and again, increasing the pressure, making love to her with his mouth, consuming her. She'd wanted this from the beginning, she realized dimly. She'd fought it, but at some level only a woman understood, she knew this was meant to be. It was foolish to deny it and futile to ignore it.

With a guttural sound, Dylan jerked his head up. They stared at each other for a long moment, their breathing ragged. Desire raged in his eyes, and his expression was filled with an intensity that took her breath away.

"I wasn't with Sam," she said softly. "Not like you think. How could I be with him when all I think about is you?"

Jessica's quiet admission was like a knife in Dylan's gut. She was the most honest open woman he'd ever met. She'd touched him like no other woman ever had, and he'd repaid that honesty with lies. If he made love to her, it would be one more lie. Not that he didn't want her, because he'd never wanted a woman as badly as he did her, but because he had nothing more to give her. There'd be no rings, no weddings, no family. All the things a woman like Jessica deserved.

He took hold of her wrists and gently pulled them away. He saw the confusion and hurt in her eyes, and it was like a hand twisting the knife already in him.

She stepped away from him, only now the hurt in her eyes was gone. In its place was anger.

"Is this a game for you, Dylan?" she said coldly. "You get your kicks from watching a woman make a fool of herself over you, then shove her away?"

He deserved every word, but they still hit with the force of a sledgehammer. He couldn't do this to her anymore. Lie to her. He had to tell her the truth, and even if she tossed him out on his butt, at least she'd know.

"Jessica," he said hoarsely, "I want to make love to you right now so badly I can't stand it." He dragged a hand through his hair and turned away, knowing he couldn't look at her without wanting to pull her back into his arms. "But your brothers..."

"Is that what this is about? My *brothers?*" She put her hand on his arm and brought him around to face her. "They might be protective, but I'm a big girl and they know it. Neither Jake nor Jared would ever interfere in my life like that. They have too much respect for me."

The hole he'd dug was getting deeper by the minute, Dylan realized. He couldn't very well tell her she was wrong, that her brothers not only *would* interfere, but they *had*. She was hurt enough. He couldn't pour salt in open wounds.

"And frankly, Dylan," she said coolly, picking up her shoes and heading for the stairs, "I'm a little surprised you're afraid of my brothers."

That did it. Something snapped inside him. She hadn't made it to the third step before he had hold of her arm, pulling her to him. "I never said I was afraid of your brothers."

Her chin lifted stubbornly. "Actions speak louder than words, Mr. Grant."

His eyes had a hard dangerous glint. "So they do."

He heard her soft gasp, and when her lips parted he plunged his tongue into the satin heat of her mouth. He felt her resistance, expected it, but it didn't sway him. He deepened the kiss, searching, seeking the passion he knew she possessed. For the second time, she dropped her shoes and flattened her palms against his chest, neither pushing him away or pulling him closer. The small sound she made in her throat turned from one of frustration to one of need. Her arms stiffened, then crept around his neck.

Relief poured through him at her acquiescence. He fitted her body to his, guiding her up the stairs with careful deliberation. She twisted against him with a moan that drove him half-mad.

Jessica's eager response sent him over the edge he'd been teetering on since the first night he'd kissed her, maybe from the first moment he'd seen her. There was only Jessica. There was only now.

The light at the top of the stairs was dim. Jessica had the sensation that she was floating, then realized that Dylan had lifted her off her feet. His large hands cupped her bottom, and he cradled her against the juncture of his legs. She felt pure feminine satisfaction at the arousal pressing urgently into her pelvis, and she moved shamelessly and erotically against the hard ridge of his manhood.

He moaned and raked his teeth over her lips, then her chin. "You keep doing that and you're going to feel this floor on your back," he growled. His mouth seared a hot trail over her jaw and her neck.

"Promises, promises," she whispered, then wound her arms more tightly around his shoulders. He chuckled softly and tasted the hollow of her neck behind her ear. Pleasure pumped through her, and she let her head fall back, urging his lips to continue their journey. He complied, branding her skin with fire-hot kisses.

The hardwood floor creaked under their combined weight, and when Dylan dipped suddenly, Jessica thought he meant to carry out his threat. Instead, he pressed her against the wall, shifting her weight as he tugged up her dress.

"Wrap your legs around me."

She wound her arms more tightly around his neck and did as he asked. His hands slid over her buttocks and her exposed thighs. He glanced down, hesitating as his fingers touched the lace tops of her nylons. He looked up at her in surprise, his eyes dark and fiercely sensual.

"I hate panty hose," she said breathlessly.

Dylan traced a finger over the edge of the soft scalloped lace that separated warm skin from silky stockings. Women's undergarments had always intrigued him, but this particular item caught him completely off guard. He was glad he hadn't known earlier. He never would have made it through the evening without dragging her off. His blood pounded in his temples, and it took every ounce of willpower he possessed not to take her right here. But he wanted to see her, to touch every inch of her before he loved her.

He felt her tremble under his touch as he moved his hand up her thigh. "What else do you hate?" he murmured,

pushing her dress up higher, wondering what other surprises she might have.

"Slow," she whispered harshly. "I hate slow."

Smiling, he moved his hands over her hips and rocked his
body against hers. Her fingers raked through his hair, then
curled tightly into his collar. She caught her lower lip between her teeth and closed her eyes. He watched the rapid
rise and fall of her chest and decided he hated slow, as well.

He lifted her higher and blazed kisses over her neck, then
downward to the swell of her breasts, frustrated by the
clothing separating them. Her fingers worked at the buttons on his shirt, and when her hands slipped inside the
fabric and touched his chest, he closed his own eyes and
swore.

Jessica smiled at the word Dylan uttered. Though she
wouldn't have expressed herself quite that way, she completely understood the feeling. Never before had she experienced such intense pleasure. Never before had a man
brought her even close to this, and she knew no other man
ever would again. No man but Dylan.

The cool wall on Jessica's back was a sharp contrast to the
hot male skin under her fingers. His muscles rippled and
bunched under her touch, and when she dragged her nails
lightly through the thicket of dark hair on his chest, she felt
his body tighten.

He brushed his lips over hers, tasting the corner of her
mouth, her cheek, her earlobe. His teeth nipped at a sensitive spot behind her ear and she drew in a breath and held
it.

"My bedroom or yours?" he murmured.

"Yours is closer."

He gathered her to him, lifting her as if she weighed no
more than a feather. They moved into his bedroom, and he
kicked the door closed behind him as he carried her to the
bed. His motions were smooth and sure, confident. A man
with a purpose, she thought with a smile.

His room was dark, but pale moonlight softly lit the room, giving shape to the shadows. There was a masculine scent here, leather and denim and musk. The night heightened her awareness, and she heard the sound of his breathing, smelled the passion in the air. His hands skimmed over her hips, then her waist as he eased her body down his until her feet touched the floor.

Her eyelids felt heavy as she lifted her gaze to his. He stared down at her with an intensity that made her shiver.

His eyes never left hers as he reached up and gently tugged the remaining pins from her hair. They bounced on the floor with tinny echoes. Her hair spilled over her shoulders.

"You're beautiful," he whispered.

She looked away, an involuntary reaction, but he cupped her face in his hands and brought her gaze back. "You have to believe that," he said, his fingers tightening almost painfully. "If nothing else, you must believe that."

She covered his hands with her own, and the rough texture sent ripples of pleasure through her. What did a woman say when a man told her with such fervency that she was beautiful? She rose on her toes and pressed her lips to his. She felt him hesitate, then his arms closed fiercely around her, and he kissed her with a recklessness that left her reeling.

She felt so small in his arms, he thought through the mist of desire. So delicate. The sound of his name on her lips empowered him. Her hands moving over his body left him weak. He found the pearl clasp at the back of her dress and opened it, then tugged the zipper down. The dress fell away, then pooled at her feet.

Dylan's breath caught. Nothing could have prepared him for the exquisite sight of her. One wisp of black lace covered her full breasts, another bridged her hips. His heart slammed in his chest. "Jessica," he whispered hoarsely, then swallowed hard.

She should have been embarrassed. Never had she stood so brazenly before any man. But it felt so right, so natural, that she could only revel in the exhilaration of his response. She leaned toward him, pressing her lips to his chest as she unbuttoned, then tugged his shirt from his pants and off his shoulders. She tasted the salt on his skin, felt the tickle of his chest hair against her cheek. His heart beat at the same erratic pace as her own, and as her hands moved lower, his sharp intake of air mixed with the rasp of a zipper.

His mouth rushed to hers with bruising force. She welcomed him, and his tongue swirled with hers over and over again. He lowered his head, then found her breast with his mouth as he cupped the soft mounds in his hands. She gasped, arching her back when he unsnapped the front clasp of her bra and drew the hardened peak of one nipple into the moist heat of his mouth.

Fire raced over her skin. An urgency built in her, almost a desperation. "Dylan, please . . ."

He seemed to ignore her, and the desperation grew to a wild writhing need. His hand moved lower and slipped under the thin strip of lace at her hips. He slid a finger slowly into the heat of her body. She trembled at the ecstasy knotting inside her.

Her knees gave way and she sank onto the bed. He followed, moving over her, his mouth on her breast, his hand stroking her most intimate spot. She bit her bottom lip and moved her head from side to side, digging her nails into his shoulders and back. "Dylan," she whimpered, "I need you. Now."

He stood and slid his own pants and briefs down in one swift movement, then fumbled in the nightstand drawer. She understood why, but the wait was unbearable until he joined her again.

The night closed around them as he lowered himself over her; their bodies were no more than silhouettes in the darkness. A man, a woman. Hard against soft. Rough against smooth. The textures of their bodies contrasted sharply, sensuously.

He knelt over her and spread her legs, entering her slowly, his hands kneading her thighs as he murmured her name. She thought she might cry from the intense pleasure consuming her. He eased himself deeper, and she buried her hands in the pillow under her head, arching her back to accept him more fully.

He moved then, and the heat spiraled through her, tightening and twisting her insides. He groaned and the sound was primitive, exciting. She clutched at the pillow, turning her face to muffle the cry that suddenly burst from her. She shuddered uncontrollably, again and again, his name on her lips. He followed her with equal force, his body convulsing as the powerful release overtook him.

It was a long while before either one of them moved. Their ragged breathing filled the night, and somewhere far in the distance a lonely coyote howled at the moon. Dylan slowly shifted his weight, rising on his elbows, but she wound her arms around his neck and pulled him back.

"I'm going to break you," he said hoarsely.

"I don't break that easily, Dylan," she murmured. "I think we both just proved that."

He didn't know what to say. He'd lost complete control and taken her like a crazed man. He *was* crazed. Her hands on his skin, her lips so eager and warm on his, had driven him over the edge. He couldn't have stopped, wouldn't have stopped, if a bulldozer had driven through the room.

He could barely make out her face in the darkness, but he saw a faint smile and heard her sigh. He ran his fingertips along her cheek, her neck, her lips. Soft. She was so soft.

Just when he thought he might bring himself back to reality, her fingers moved lazily over his arms, then down his back. Reality could wait, he thought dimly, pressing his mouth to hers and kissing her deeply. It wasn't going any-

where, he knew that, and there was nothing more impera-
tive at this moment than the woman in his arms.

Jessica took her time exploring the hard planes and val-
leys of Dylan's back with her fingertips. A fine sheen of
perspiration covered his body—both their bodies—and her
hands slid smoothly over his damp skin. Dylan's lips moved
insistently over hers, and she answered the kiss with equal
persuasion.

She knew she should be embarrassed by her lack of inhi-
bition, but she was too thoroughly content to care at the
moment. She'd save her shyness for the light, for the morning that was sure to come, bringing with it regret. The
thought gave her a sharp pain in her chest, but she quickly
pushed it away. She wouldn't think about the morning. She
wanted only to think about now, about the man who held
her as if she was the most precious thing in the world.

His chin scraped over her cheek, her neck, her shoulder.
Her fingers slid over his shoulders, his waist, his hips. As his
mouth moved lower, so did her hands. Skin that had begun
to cool, heated again. There was a gentleness in his touch
that surprised her, a slow tenderness that picked her up and
pulled her along like a leaf in the breeze.

The urgency rose, but still he moved with precision,
slowly, sensuously. She began to squirm, then writhe, and
still he moved as leisurely if he was taking a Sunday stroll.
She wanted to curse him, to shout at him. Her body ached,
and his unhurried pace became a sweet torture. An unbearable torture.

She dug her hands in his hair and arched her body upward.

"Dylan!"

Was this really possible? So soon? She cried out again and
he met her fully, completely, dragging her tightly to him with
a deep groan. She clung to him, gasping as the shudders
overtook her.

And in the quiet afterward, she curled into Dylan's arms and drew the darkness around her as she would a blanket, wishing that morning would never come.

Lucas and Meggie sat on the steps of the church, looking up at the stars. Hannibal lay beside them, head on his paws, dozing intermittently. The moon glowed silver, illuminating Meggie's slender form.

Strange, Lucas thought, how Meggie still made his breath catch and his heart beat faster. Who would have thought that a ghost had such feelings? It was torture to be able to feel all the emotions of a living man, but unable to do anything about them. Still, he would rather experience the pain of the feelings than have no feelings at all.

Meggie glanced over at the hotel and sighed. "Are they up there together?" she asked.

He nodded. Meggie had been in the church, but he'd been in the hotel, waiting with Dylan for Jessica to get home tonight. He'd rather enjoyed the argument, but when Dylan kissed Jessica, Lucas, as any gentleman would, had left. A man and a woman about to make love certainly did not need company, not even a ghost's. Hannibal had thought it best to come along with him.

"Are they making love?"

Lucas shifted uncomfortably. He and Meggie rarely talked of things like this. Until now, there'd really been no reason to. "It would seem likely."

Her expression grew pensive. "I wish we had made love, Lucas. I want so much to know how it would have felt to be with you like that. How I wish we hadn't waited."

"We were from another time, Meggie. Opinions of things like that were quite different, if you remember."

She shook her head sadly. "We were wrong. I can't imagine anything more beautiful than making love with someone you love." Meggie sighed and glanced up at the hotel, then back to Lucas. "Do you think we'll ever know that kind of love?"

"Perhaps," he said quietly. "Or perhaps we will experience a greater love, a joining that reaches far beyond that of the physical."

Meggie smiled at the thought and held up her hand. He brought up his hand, as well, matching his fingers to hers. He felt an energy he'd never felt before, almost a sensation of skin touching skin. Stunned, he looked at Meggie, whose eyes had grown wide. She felt it, also. Was it possible?

They stared in amazement at each other, then smiled slowly.

Eight

Something woke him.

Dylan opened his eyes and squinted at the sunlight pouring through the window. He blinked several times and listened.

There it was again. Sort of a high-pitched whine. In fact, it *was* a high-pitched whine. Just outside the bedroom door. He rose on one elbow, then realized what it was.

Hannibal.

Shaking his head, he smiled and lay back down. His smile slowly faded as he stared at the woman lying beside him. His breath caught in his throat.

She slept on her side with one hand curled under her chin. Her hair, tousled from sleep, lay in wisps around her face, and her lips were rosy and swollen from their lovemaking. Looking at her aroused him instantly; his entire body ached with wanting her.

Dammit, anyway! What the hell have I done?

He moved the covers slowly, intending to slip out of bed, but she stirred, then looked at him from beneath sleep-heavy lids. Her eyes, deep, deep blue, held him like velvet chains. When she reached out and lightly traced her fingers over his shoulder, he groaned silently, knowing he was trapped. She'd hate him soon enough, he thought as he slid back down under the covers and gathered her close. Too soon. He'd deal with his conscience later.

"Mornin'," she said huskily.

"Morning."

Hannibal whined again.

"I've spoiled him," Jessica said, skimming her finger-nails over Dylan's chest. "He's used to sleeping by my bed every night."

It would be easy to let himself be spoiled by Jessica, Dylan thought, though sleeping *in* her bed every night, rather than by it, would be more to his liking. "Should we let him in?"

With a soft sigh, Jessica slid one long silken leg over his. "Not just yet," she murmured.

That was all it took. One touch, and the madness came over him again. He pulled her roughly beneath him, whispering her name, holding her gaze with his own as he entered her. Cheeks flushed, lips parted, she eagerly responded until the madness came over them both.

And as the beating of their hearts slowed, Jessica knew with painful clarity the instant reality took hold of Dylan. She sensed his sudden awkwardness, his hesitation. As if he wanted to say something, to explain, but hadn't the words.

She'd thought last night she could handle morning regrets. That she was a mature, reasonable woman who could deal with whatever the new day brought. But what it had brought was so unexpected, so earth-shattering, that all she wanted to do was crawl under the covers and wail like a baby.

She wasn't going to make a fool of herself. At least, no more than she already had. She'd make it easy on him. On both of them. She forced a smile and slid out of Dylan's arms.

"So, how about some breakfast?" She sat on the edge of the bed and searched frantically for something to cover herself with. Anything to feel less vulnerable. Her dress was out of reach so she grabbed for his shirt and tugged it on. "Eggs or pancakes? The sausage is frozen, but I could—"

"Jessica."

The somber tone of his voice only tightened the knot in her heart. He took her arm and pulled her closer.

"Jess," he said more softly, using a nickname only her family ever used, "look at me."

She didn't want to. She already heard the regret in his voice. She couldn't stand to see it in his eyes, as well. "Dylan, it's all right. It's the wedding. Everyone just sort of gets caught up in the excitement, you know. It happens all the time."

"Not to me," he said. "And I don't think to you, either. Last night was special to me, I want you to believe that. *You* are special."

"I don't need a line, Dylan. There's no one standing here with a shotgun. Not even my brothers, though I doubt they'd be thrilled."

She saw that look in his eyes again. A strange mixture of anger and guilt at the mention of Jake and Jared. Frowning, she turned and faced him in disbelief. "Is that what your sudden remorse is all about? My brothers?"

"This is ridiculous." Jaw tight, he sat on the edge of the bed and grabbed for his jeans.

She turned away as he tugged on his pants. But he hadn't answered her question. "What, did they threaten you or something?"

He rolled his eyes and swore. "Nobody threatened me. And I told you, I'm not afraid of your brothers."

Arms folded, she stood and faced him. "Then what are you afraid of? We spend one night together, one simple night, and you act as if I've got the preacher man standing on the other side of the door."

Eyes narrowed, he took hold of her shoulders and hauled her against him. "You can believe what you want, Jessica, but believe this. There was nothing, *nothing,* simple about last night. And as far as your brothers go, there is one thing we agree on. None of us wants to see you get hurt."

Too late, she thought, refusing to give in to the threatening tears. She pushed away from him, and her skin burned where he'd touched her. "You don't have to worry about me, Dylan," she said with slow precision. "You aren't the only one who learns from mistakes. I think we can both view this as an educational experience."

She gathered her clothing and headed for the door on legs the consistency of warm molasses. "I'll return your shirt later," she said as casually as if they were friends borrowing clothes. When she opened the door, Hannibal bounded in with a loud bark.

"On second thought—" she tugged the garment from her shoulders and tossed it on the floor "—you can keep it."

His mouth was still open when she quietly closed the door.

"Son of a bitch!"

Dylan continued to swear as the pain ricocheted up his hand and through his arm. Jaws clenched, he turned away from the window frame he'd been nailing in the church and kicked his toolbox.

Jessica, who was painting the frames, glanced over, but never missed a stroke with her brush. The rest of the crew paused, then continued with their work. They'd grown accustomed to Dylan's irascible temper the past few days.

He had good reason to be angry, he told himself. Everything that *could* have gone wrong since the week started *had* gone wrong. The lumber company lost a shipping order of studs that Dylan needed three days ago, there was an electrical short somewhere in the church wiring that had yet to be found, and the brand-new plumbing had mysteriously backed up. Everything was taking longer than it should and costing more.

And now his thumb hurt like hell.

He'd been thinking about Jessica when the hammer had slipped. But then, it was rare he *wasn't* thinking about Jessica. Not just that incredible night they'd spent together, but that provocative manner she'd left him in the morning. If she'd intended revenge, it had certainly worked. Not a minute went by that he didn't think about her. Her scent still lingered on his pillow, in his room, even on the shirt she'd so casually shrugged out of as she'd walked out. He hadn't had a decent night's sleep since.

He was glad he hit his thumb. It was a hell of a lot easier to deal with an aching thumb than the other part of his anatomy that was in pain.

But what really got him, he thought as he ground his back teeth, was her casual dismissal of that night. She'd never mentioned it once and had acted as if nothing at all had happened. They still had their meals together, worked together. They'd even ridden into town together to pick up some supplies.

She was making him crazy.

Just for good measure he kicked his toolbox again.

Temporarily appeased, he let out a long breath and glanced around the church. It was almost finished. They would install the windows today and put a final coat of paint on the walls. Then all he had to do was find that damn short in the wiring and they were done here. He knew how much Jessica wanted the church ready for Christmas, and he was determined it would be.

He watched as Dean sneaked in the back door of the church. He had on a cowboy hat and kept his head down as he took over for one of the other kids nailing frames. Last week he'd been the most eager and experienced worker on the crew; Dylan had even put him in charge. But he hadn't shown up yesterday, or called, and now he was late.

Even seventeen-year-olds needed to find out what the real workplace was like, Dylan thought as he headed for the young man. If the kid couldn't cut it, then he'd better hit the road.

"Have a hard time getting yourself out of bed the past couple of days?" Arms folded, Dylan stood behind the latecomer.

"Sorry," Dean muttered, but didn't turn around.

"A job is a responsibility. If you aren't here, we all have to work harder." Dylan knew he was preaching, the same way his bosses had preached at him when he'd done something stupid.

"I said I was sorry." Dean's shoulders were stiff as he swung the hammer.

Dylan frowned. Dean had always been cool, but never rude. Dylan put a hand on his arm. "Look, Dean—"

The kid swung around then, his mouth tight as he raised the hammer. "Don't touch me."

Dylan stared at the young man and froze. His face was black-and-blue, one eye nearly swollen shut. "Good Lord, what happened?"

Dean lowered his gaze and the hammer at the same time. His shoulders slumped. "Nothing."

When Dylan touched his shoulder, Dean jerked away, but Dylan wouldn't be put off. He nodded to the back door. "Let's go."

Resigned to his fate, Dean trudged outside, Dylan behind him. "Have you seen a doctor?" he asked.

Dean shook his head. "I haven't got money for that."

"What about your parents?"

A dry laugh caught in Dean's throat. "My mom's been dead for three years. My dad only has money for booze."

A sick feeling twisted Dylan's gut. "And this is what happens when he has too much of that?"

The teenager shrugged. "It don't matter 'bout me. I could leave. But I got a kid brother who's gonna get it next if I can't get the money to get us both out of there." Dean looked down at the ground. "Don't fire me," he said. "Please."

White-hot anger filled Dylan, a furious rage that any man could do this to his own child, or to any child. He'd like to pay the man a call, let the coward face someone who could defend himself. "Who the hell said anything about firing you? You've got the most experience of the crew, and I need every man I have."

Relief eased Dean's shoulders. "I'll stay late tonight to make up time. My brother's with a neighbor while school's out."

"Tomorrow. Right now I want you to get back into town and see the doctor. Have the bill sent here in my name. We have a medical account that'll cover it, plus any time lost at work. If you can, be here in the morning."

Dean nodded and started to leave. Then he turned back and stuck out his hand. "Thanks, Dylan," he said quietly. "You're okay."

Surprised at the swelling he felt in his chest, Dylan shook the young man's hand. "Now get out of here. I've got to get back to work."

Dean grinned, then drove off in his battered pickup. Dylan stared after the truck until all he saw was dust. When he turned, Jessica stood at the back door of the church, watching him intently.

"Since when do we have a medical or time-lost account?" she asked, lifting one brow.

"Take it out of my pay."

"Better watch out, Dylan," she said with a smile. "I think 'do-gooder' just crept onto your application. Before you know it, 'volunteer' will be right next to it."

He frowned at her.

Would she ever figure this man out? Jessica wondered, trying to deal with the emotions skittering through her at the moment. She'd spent the past four days convincing herself he was a complete cad and she was glad nothing had developed from their making love.

Then she had to witness that one brief exchange between him and Dean. He hadn't embarrassed the teenager. He'd treated the young man with respect and kindness. A lot of men would have backed away, closed their eyes and their minds. He hadn't.

And the wall she'd so carefully built came tumbling down.

Damn you, Dylan Grant!

He moved toward her and gestured in the direction Dean had left. "How long has that been going on?"

"Mostly since his mother died. I was in Dallas working in social services at the time, but I understand his dad started drinking heavily, and there was no one to take his anger out on except Dean. So far he hasn't hit Troy, Dean's nine-year-old brother, but it's just a matter of time."

"A matter of time?" Dylan stared at her in disbelief. "Why the hell hasn't anyone put the bastard away?"

She sighed heavily. "Dean would deny it if it went to court. It might be hard to believe, but he still loves his dad. He understands that's his father's way of dealing with his grief."

"By hitting his own kid?"

"I've seen worse." She stared blankly past him. "Every one of these kids here, and the rest in town, has his, or her, own story. If I can help even one of them, then every penny spent here on Makeshift—" she glanced down at his hand and smiled "—and every smashed thumb is worth it."

Dylan felt as if he'd lived his entire life in a closed-up house, and suddenly, for the first time, all the windows and doors were thrown open. He understood now why she wanted to help these kids. Give them a chance no one else had. "What can I do?"

Her gaze flicked to his. "You mean help?"

Why did she have to look so damn surprised? he thought irritably. "Yes."

"You just did," she said quietly. "You listened to Dean, but you made no judgment, gave no lecture. He'll trust you now. There's nothing more important than that."

Trust. The word stuck like a rock in Dylan's throat. When had all this gotten so complicated? If the road to hell was truly paved with good intentions, he was well on his way.

He'd had enough of this. He was done lying.

Somewhere, at the other end of town, Dylan heard Hannibal barking insistently, but he ignored the dog. He took Jessica by the arm and dragged her away from the back door of the church where anyone else might hear. "We need to talk," he said tersely.

Brow furrowed, she stared at him. He hadn't a clue what to say. "Jessica—"

She lifted a hand to cut him off, turning her head as she listened to Hannibal's bark. Her eyes narrowed suddenly. "Dylan," she said slowly, fearfully. "Something's wrong."

Something *was* wrong, he realized. Hannibal's bark demanded attention.

"Oh, my God! Dylan!" She looked over his shoulder. "No!"

He spun around, and his heart jumped into his throat.

Smoke billowed from the saloon.

"Fire!" he screamed to the crew. He was already running for the saloon with Jessica at his heels as the kids spilled out of the church. "Get the extinguishers," he yelled over his shoulder.

Jessica's mind raced, and she felt as if she was moving in slow motion. Thick black smoke poured from the saloon's double swinging doors. Hannibal was backing away from them, barking at the billowing cloud as if it were a living creature.

It was her greatest fear. An uncontrolled fire could destroy Makeshift in minutes. In his blueprints, Dylan had included a complete system of alarms and sprinklers, but there'd been no time yet to install them. As a precaution, though, every building had at least two extinguishers.

She couldn't lose it all now, not when she was so close. She started to run into the saloon, but a pair of strong arms grabbed her roughly and hauled her back.

"Where do you think you're going?" Dylan yelled.

"I've got to get in there," she yelled back, trying to pull away from him. Smoke curled around them, burning her eyes, and the sound of flames crackled from inside the building.

He held her tightly. "The hell you do."

Larry and Pete ran up, carrying extinguishers. She stumbled backward as Dylan let go of her and grabbed one of the cans. "Don't come in unless I call for you," he said to the two young men, then gestured at Jessica. "And if she takes one step closer, lock her in the jailhouse."

They nodded, then looked at her apologetically.

Furious, she watched helplessly as Dylan drew a deep breath and dove through the black cloud. She heard the squall of the extinguisher and the heavy stomp of boots. The smoke intensified.

The rest of the crew showed up, all of them carrying extinguishers they'd gathered from other buildings. They stood in a line, quietly watching, waiting for a sign from Dylan. Even Hannibal had stopped barking and sat watching, his head tilted as he stared into the saloon.

Jessica's fear turned to panic.

"Dylan!"

No answer. She started to move toward the doors, but the boys grabbed her. *"Dylan!"*

She struggled, calling his name. The fire, and what it might do to Makeshift, no longer mattered to her. Dylan was all that mattered. She twisted sharply away from her captors, catching them off guard, then ran straight through the doors and smack into Dylan's wide chest. His arms came around her. Coughing, he lifted her off the ground and dragged her back outside into the middle of the street.

"Dylan!" She pressed her cheek against his chest. "Thank God."

"I thought I told you to stay outside," he said hoarsely, gasping as he drew in air.

"You have a lot to learn about me, Dylan Grant, if you think I can be bossed around so easily." She stepped back and ran her hands over his arms, checking him for burns. Soot smeared his face and clothes, and the smell of smoke clung to him. "Are you all right?"

He nodded. "I caught it before any serious flames could get started. A few more minutes, though, and the place would've gone up like dry kindling."

Hannibal nudged his way between them, licking Dylan's hand. Jessica knelt down and hugged the dog. "Thank you, boy. You and Dylan saved the town." She looked up at the others. "You were all terrific. If you hadn't moved so fast, we could have lost Makeshift."

They all grinned, then shifted modestly. "You know what caused it?" Pete asked.

Dylan shook his head. "Not yet. Once the smoke clears, I'll check it out. You can all get back to work now. I'll take care of things here."

Excitement over, the boys shuffled back to the church. Jessica's heart was still pounding hard as she faced Dylan again. She wanted to wrap her arms around his neck and pull him close, but the tight expression she saw on his face stopped her. She slipped her hands into the back pockets of her jeans, instead. "Are you sure you're all right?"

"What were you thinking?" he said tightly. "A roof could've collapsed. The smoke could've gotten you. Dammit," he said, his voice softening, "you could've been hurt."

Surprised by the concern in his voice, Jessica went still. She felt the heavy thud of her heart as she lifted her gaze to his. "I wasn't hurt."

"Maybe not this time," he said, his eyes searching her face.

"What do you mean, not this time?"

"I mean—" his lips thinned and he stepped closer "—this was no accident."

She couldn't sleep. She heard the steady tick of her bed-side clock, Hannibal's deep breathing, the persistent creak-ing common to all old buildings.

The sounds were magnified tonight, as was her aware-ness of the man sleeping in the room next to hers. She couldn't erase the image of him running into the smoke, the seconds that felt like hours when he hadn't come back out. Her heart still slammed in her chest every time she thought of what might have happened if the fire had been more se-rious.

This was no accident.

Dylan's words still pounded in her brain. The thought of someone intentionally starting a fire was inconceivable. She couldn't believe it. She refused to believe it.

With a heavy sigh, she slipped out of bed, tugged on her robe, then quietly made her way down the stairs. She could have used a flashlight or turned on one of the lights Dylan had installed in the hallway, but she preferred the darkness. Even as a child she'd never been afraid of the dark. She'd always found a comfort in the quiet blanket of night. That was when she could see the stars, and here in Makeshift, there were millions of them.

She moved silently into the kitchen, closing the door behind her as she fumbled for the light.

A hand reached out and grabbed her, then threw her against the wall.

Nine

"**D**ylan!"

Heart pounding, Jessica realized it was Dylan who held her securely against the wall. She felt his hard body press against hers, heard the sound of his rapid breathing, then a muttered curse as he loosened his grip. Still, he did not release her completely, and she let her body slump.

"You scared me to death!" she said, breathless.

"What are you doing sneaking around in the dark?" he asked.

He gripped her wrists more tightly, pinning her to the wall. The coarse texture of his hands on her skin sent shivers up her spine.

Either one of them could have pulled away and turned on a light. They didn't. They stood there, torso to torso, his face inches from hers.

She couldn't see him in the blackness, but she'd never been more aware of a man in her life. The darkness did that, she thought dimly. Changed a person's focus. In the darkness there was nothing but feelings, a honing of the senses. Her pulse raced, her skin tightened. His breath was like a warm feather skimming her neck, and she caught the faint scent of whiskey.

"Having a little midnight nip?" She forced a light tone into her voice. She felt more than saw his answering smile. She held her breath as he moved closer, bringing his lips a whisper from hers.

"A little nip never hurt anyone," he murmured.

Anticipation shimmered through her as his mouth hovered close. With a will of their own, her lips parted and her eyes slowly closed.

Dylan felt Jessica's body soften against his, felt the rise and fall of her breasts. A hunger consumed him that neither food nor drink could ever quench. Only *she* could. When he actually considered pressing his lips to hers, Dylan knew he'd had too much to drink. Or perhaps too little.

He released her slowly, then flicked on the light. They both blinked.

"Sorry," he muttered, stepping away and shoving a hand through his hair. "I'm a little edgy tonight."

She pulled her robe tightly around her. "Because of today?"

Because of today. Because of her. Because she could have been hurt in the fire and the thought terrified him. That was what had driven him down here. His fear. That she might yet be hurt. If not by someone else, then most certainly by him.

"Those oil-soaked rags didn't get in that saloon by accident, Jessica." He eased down into a chair at the table where a shot glass sat beside a whiskey bottle.

"They could've been there a long time." She took the chair beside him. "Maybe the weather or the humidity set them off. Or maybe an animal dragged them in to set up a nest."

He shook his head. "I can't believe that."

"Dylan, none of my kids would've done anything like that. There has to be another explanation."

"We already went over all this at dinner. And I never said the kids did it."

She still didn't want to believe it. "So who, then?"

"If I knew, I sure as hell wouldn't be sitting here. I'd have my fist in someone's face."

He refilled the shot glass and held it out to her. Their fingers touched as she took the drink from him.

"My mother used to make me hot chocolate with little marshmallows when I couldn't sleep." She stared at the glass.

"Somehow," he drawled, "I can't quite picture marshmallows in whiskey, but I'll try to rustle some up for you if it helps."

She looked at him, and the crooked grin on his face had her smiling. "Maybe next time."

Somehow she knew there wouldn't be very many next times with Dylan. He'd made it clear he wasn't a man who stayed put.

"Tell me about your mother," he asked quietly.

She took a sip of the whiskey and grimaced. "She was a beautiful woman, small and slender. My brothers and father towered over her, but she only had to give a look and they toed the line. My father worshiped her. Her death devastated him."

"And you?"

A heartbeat of silence passed between them. "I adored her. She always knew the right thing to say and when to say it. I missed that when she was gone. She used to wake me every morning and say, 'Wake up, Jess, it's a beautiful day.'" She stared at the glass in her hand. "It didn't matter if there was a thunderstorm, she always said the same thing, 'Wake up, Jess,'" she repeated softly, "'it's a beautiful day.'"

It had been a long time since she'd thought about that. And though the words brought an ache to her chest and moisture to her eyes, there was comfort in them, as well. "I was angry after that. Angry because everyone had lied to me about her dying. Angry because she was gone. Angry my father married another woman. My grades dropped and I started to hang with different kids. I was sneaking out at night, coming home late."

Dylan took the glass from her hand and downed the remaining liquor, then refilled it and pressed it back into her fingers. "You turned out okay. Better than okay," he added with a grin.

She tucked her hair behind her ears and smiled. "There was a big question over the issue in that period of my life. I spent a lot of time here at Makeshift. It was my own special place. Even as a child I'd felt good here, that I belonged here." Her smiled faded. "But I came here with the wrong kids. Before I knew it, they were bringing alcohol here, and drugs."

Dylan watched Jessica's eyes narrow as she remembered. "One of the guys, Tim, brought some marijuana, and another one, Bobby, a bottle of vodka. I was too stupid to realize what they were up to, but after I had a few sips of alcohol, I caught on real quick. I tried to get away from them, but they were stronger than me."

Dylan felt as if a fist were squeezing his chest. He tensed, waiting to hear what happened, yet not wanting to hear.

"What they had in mind," she continued, "wasn't what I intended at all. I started to panic. All I could think about was how disappointed my mother would be. How disappointed I was in myself."

Dylan barely managed to contain the rage that poured through his body. She held his gaze, though he suspected she wasn't truly looking at him.

"And then the most incredible thing happened," she said. "I wasn't afraid anymore. I stopped struggling, calmly

looked at both of them and told them if they didn't let go of
me they'd be sorry. Of course they only laughed.''

She smiled slowly. ''Then, as if someone was lifting my
arm for me, I swung my fist and hit Tim. He flew across the
room and smashed into the wall. Stunned, Bobby just stood
there. I simply touched him, one finger to his chest, and it
sent him sprawling. Gave him a broken nose.''

Dylan frowned at her. ''I don't understand.''

She leaned closer. ''It's what I've been trying to tell you,
Dylan. It was Lucas. He wouldn't let anyone hurt me. He's
always been here for me. That's why I'm not afraid here.
And that's why I've got to build this center. For all those
kids who need a place to go, to be with someone who understands. Someone who can whisper each morning, 'Wake
up, it's a beautiful day,' even when it's not.''

Dylan could only stare. He tried to speak, but the words
wouldn't come. Her eyes were midnight blue, dark with
earnestness. He had no idea what to make of her story, but
he knew she believed it from the depths of her heart. He
wanted to believe, too, but it was so incredible, so far-
fetched, reason refused to accept it.

But there was no reason with this woman. Only the sweet
sensation of her compelling beauty, inside and out, drawing him closer even as he pulled away.

Setting the glass down, he gave in to the need to touch her
and took her hand in his. It was cool and soft in his palm.
''Jessica, if someone is trying to undermine this project, you
aren't safe here.''

She tensed at his words, but her eyes held his. ''You're
here,'' she said quietly.

Frustration and desire had him aching for her. That she
would trust him like that, look to him for safety, brought
forth a fierce primitive need to protect, to shelter this
woman from any person who might harm her.

He'd almost told her the truth earlier, before the fire had
stopped him. And now the time was hardly right. As if the

time would ever be right, he thought with a sigh. He had to talk to Jake and Jared as soon as possible, but with Jared on his honeymoon, that wouldn't be until Christmas.

He realized how tightly he was holding her hand and released it. "And what if I wasn't here?" he asked.

A long moment passed between them. Then she blinked slowly and straightened with a shrug. "I managed before you came here, Dylan. I'll manage after you've gone."

The truth of her words, spoken with such cool indifference, had him grinding his teeth. He wanted to shake her. He wanted to kiss her senseless and drag her upstairs.

But he *would* be leaving. They both knew that. It was wrong to pretend otherwise. "And how exactly do you plan to *manage* if someone decides this town ain't big enough for the two of you?"

"I've got Hannibal."

He rolled his eyes and shook his head. "You expect a dog to protect you out here in the middle of nowhere?"

"I seem to recall it was Hannibal who warned us about the fire this afternoon. We'd be sitting in ashes right now if it wasn't for him." She stood, her shoulders rigid as she faced him. "But the fact is, what I do or don't expect is really no concern of yours, Dylan. And while I admit that some of my decisions may be bad ones, they're still my decisions. I'll live with the consequences."

His fingers tightened around the glass in his hand. He knew she was talking about him now, about the night they'd made love. She'd neatly labeled him in the category of "bad decisions." And while he understood, he sure as hell didn't like it.

"That's what I want to make sure of, Jessica." He lifted his glass to his lips and downed the contents. "That you live, consequences or not."

The church was finished Christmas Eve day. Late-afternoon sun streamed in through the new leaded windows, and the freshly varnished pews and floor shone brightly. Jessica set the pair of crystal candle holders that had been her great-grandmother's on the altar, then draped a pine bough over the corners.

"Merry Christmas, Lucas and Meggie," she whispered, and stood back to admire the church. A sudden breeze floated through the room, stirring the crystal teardrops on the candlesticks and creating a tinkly musical sound. Jessica smiled. "You're welcome."

Humming "Here Comes Santa Claus," she turned and headed for the hotel, where the crew had gone ahead to wash up for eggnog, punch and sodas. She'd also made popcorn and holiday cookies, and wrapped a small gift for each of the kids. They'd worked hard to finish the church by Christmas, and she appreciated it more than she could say.

But none had worked harder than Dylan. Other than brief meals where strained silence had prevailed, she'd barely seen him since that night in the kitchen. And while she suspected that his diligence had a great deal to do with avoiding her, she also wanted to believe that he'd put in the extra hours because he, too, had wanted to see the church completed by tomorrow, and that Makeshift had become more than just another job to him.

Or that she'd become more than just another woman.

It was a dangerous thought, she knew. Dylan had made it clear he had no intention of staying on here. If she let herself fantasize that his physical attraction might grow into anything beyond that, she was setting herself up for the fall of a lifetime. She knew instinctively that once she gave her heart to Dylan, there'd be no turning back.

But she wanted marriage and a family, not a casual affair. Her plans did not include pining away for a lost love. It would take her some time to forget him, but she would, she resolved, though the ache in her chest argued with her. She'd have a wedding here in Makeshift in the church he'd rebuilt, and she'd have children.

She'd nearly reached the hotel when Hannibal came bounding down the sidewalk. He barked sharply when he saw her, then turned and headed back to the hotel. He stopped at the doorway, barked again, then disappeared inside.

Frowning, Jessica followed the dog. No doubt he wanted a cookie. The beast hadn't taken his eyes off the tray when she'd pulled it out of the oven.

When she stepped into the hotel lobby, her breath caught. The boys all stood around a Christmas tree that nearly touched the twelve-foot ceiling. There were no decorations on the tree, but the branches were full and green and the scent of pine filled the hotel. She stared at the tree, then looked at the young men. They were all grinning to beat the band. Dylan stood off to the side, his arms folded and a crooked smile on his face.

Larry took a step forward and jammed his hands into his pockets. "We knew you didn't have time to get out for a tree, so we all pitched in and bought you one. Sorry there's no decorations. We sort of forgot about that."

"It's beautiful," she whispered, and reached out to touch one fragrant branch. "I don't know what to say."

"It was Dean's idea," Pete said, nudging the dark-haired kid.

Jessica smiled at the blush on Dean's face. "Thank you. All of you."

Tony pulled out a twig of mistletoe and, with a big grin, held it over his head. Laughing, Jessica kissed each boy on the cheek as the mistletoe was passed around. She hesitated when Pete handed the twig to Dylan.

"Go on, Jessica," the kids taunted. "Dylan helped set the tree up, too."

His dark gaze met hers, almost daring her, and the smile on his lips was challenging. She rose on tiptoe to place a kiss on his cheek, but he turned at the last minute and swooped down on her, circling her with his arms as he slanted his mouth against hers. The boys cheered and whistled, then clapped when Dylan finally released her.

She felt her face burn. And though his kiss infuriated her, it had also aroused her. That infuriated her all the more.

She frowned at him. "Punch?" she said, then turned away and headed for the eggnog, wishing there was something stronger that might settle her nerves.

She passed out her presents, and each of the kids thanked her as if she'd given them a new car. When she handed Dylan a package, as well, his look was one of astonishment. He hesitated a moment, almost unsure of what to do, then ripped opened the paper and pulled out the leather gloves she'd bought him. She felt her stomach flutter when he looked back at her with a smile as wide as the boys'.

They ate cookies and popcorn, and when it was time to go, they all hugged her and wished her a merry Christmas.

Dean was the last to leave. He held the baseball cap Jessica had given him in his hands, plus a present she'd bought for his little brother. He cleared his throat and stared awkwardly at the floor. "I appreciate all you've done for me, Jessica. Anything I can ever do for you, you just say so."

She hugged the young man. "You get an education, then come back here and work for me."

He smiled, then turned to Dylan. "You ready to go?"

Go? She looked at Dylan, who glanced at her, then nodded to Dean. "You go on. I'll take my bike and meet you in town."

When Dean left, she turned to Dylan. "You aren't going to Jake's with me?"

He shook his head. "I'm sorry, Jess. Dean mentioned his dad was going to a party tonight, so I thought I'd hang out in town with Dean and his brother."

He was worried about Dean and Troy, Jessica realized. He wasn't going to come out and say it, but she knew that was why he was going. He was afraid that Dean's dad would come home drunk, and he didn't want to see any harm come to the kids.

Her chest swelled with emotion. Would she ever understand this man? Outside, he had an edge as hard as a diamond. But inside, where it really mattered, where he let few people see, he had a quiet compassion, a tenderness she doubted even he'd admit to.

She felt a twinge—no, more like a stab—of disappointment that he hadn't asked her along, but she understood. He had no ties here, no family. But she did. If she came along, Dean would feel as if he was being baby-sat.

Forcing a smile, she glanced up at him. "Somebody must have tipped you off that Savannah had Christmas carols planned. You're off the hook now."

"Jessica—" he stared at the gloves in his hand "—I won't be back here tonight."

Her disappointment settled into a hollow ache. "I'll be fine, Dylan. You go on."

He looked at her for a moment, started to say something, then mumbled, "Thanks again for the gloves," and left.

The room was silent when he closed the door behind him and she was alone. Christmas Eve had always been a time of magic, a special night of anticipation, of excitement. A time to share with those you love.

And as she listened to the sound of Dylan's bike driving away, her heart felt as empty as the branches on her tree.

The smell of mesquite filled the crisp air when Dylan returned from Cactus Flat later that night. His tires crunched gravel on the road beneath him; above him, the full moon shone silver and thousands of stars sprinkled the sky.

He'd passed through West Texas several times in his life, but he'd never noticed how beautiful it was here. He'd never seen bluer skies or wider spaces. Stone Creek was an exceptional place. He understood why it was important to all the

Stone siblings, why they held on so fiercely to the land. There was no amount of money that could buy what J. T. Stone had left his children.

He cut his engine and coasted into Makeshift, then frowned at the sight of Jessica's truck parked in front of the hotel. She was supposed to be at Jake and Savannah's tonight, celebrating Christmas Eve. She wouldn't have missed spending the evening with her family.

Unless something was wrong.

His body tensed at that thought, and a sliver of fear crept through him. He parked his bike and moved quietly toward the hotel. If there was a problem or if someone was there who shouldn't be, he sure as hell didn't want that someone to know he'd come back to town.

Through the leaded windows of the hotel-lobby door, Dylan saw the glow of a soft light. It almost appeared to be moving. A flashlight? he wondered, slowly opening the door.

His heart hammered as he stepped silently inside.

As he realized what the light was, his breath caught.

Ten

There were candles everywhere. Surrounding the tree, on the lobby counter, at the foot of the stairs. Flames jumped and flickered, shadows danced on the walls. The scent of pine and wax filled the air, along with the sound of "Waltz of the Sugarplum Fairies."

Jessica sat cross-legged on an antique rug in the middle of the floor, Indian style, with a pillow propped behind her. Her dress was white lace, with a high collar and long fitted sleeves and waist. Her dark hair shone in the wavering light and hung loose over her shoulders and down her back.

His throat went dry. It was impossible to move. All he could do was stare. *Breathe,* he reminded himself.

A long strand of popcorn lay over her skirt and across the floor. Captivated, he watched as her slender fingers pulled a needle through each puff. He realized she was making garlands, and as he glanced at the tree, he saw she'd already draped several around the branches. Star and bell cookies, with red ribbons, hung beside them.

It was like something out of a Victorian storybook. A child's fairy tale. He half expected her to disappear like one of her ghosts, but when she began to hum, he knew she was real.

He closed the door, and the soft click of the latch brought her head up.

"Dylan!" Her eyes widened with surprise. "What are you doing here?"

"Dean and his brother spent the night with a friend." He knelt down beside her. "But I might ask you the same question. I thought you were going to Jake's."

She finger-combed her hair away from her face and met his gaze. Her eyes were like glittering blue ice in the candle-light. "I got so caught up here I lost track of the time. I called Jake and told him I'd see them all tomorrow."

Dylan glanced around at the shimmering lights. "Where'd you get all these?"

"They're my emergency candles," she said with a smile. "It was tradition in Makeshift to leave candles burning on special occasions. Besides, Christmas Eve and no decorations on the tree is an emergency in my book." She waved a hand toward the tree. "So what do you think?"

He leaned back and looked at the tree. "I think it's a good thing we didn't have egg rolls or carrot sticks earlier."

Laughing, she threw a piece of popcorn at him. "Be serious."

He tossed the popcorn in his mouth and chewed thoughtfully as he stared at her masterpiece. "I think it's the most beautiful tree I've ever seen."

Her eyes darkened with pleasure. "You're just saying that."

"So like a woman." He shook his head. "Fish for a compliment, then turn your nose up when you get one."

She lifted her chin indignantly. "I wasn't fishing."

He raised one brow.

"Well, so maybe I was," she admitted, threading her needle though several more kernels of popped corn. "But we women wouldn't have to hint around if men would just come out and say something nice without prompting. Try it sometime."

"A compliment without prompting?" Dylan shook his head. "There are rules against that."

"It's Christmas Eve." She set her needle down. "Break the rules."

Break the rules.

Her words, though spoken innocently, made his pulse begin to pound. *Break the rules.* That was exactly what he wanted to do. Break every damn one of them.

He looked at her, at the soft sparkle of light in her hair and her eyes. He felt a sudden ache, a longing so intense that his breath caught. Unable to resist, he reached out and touched the top pearl button at the base of her collar. It felt smooth and satiny. The way her skin did.

"I like this dress." His finger slid down to the next button.

"It was my great-grandmother Sarah's," she said, her voice breathless. "I was getting dressed to go to Jake's when the strangest impulse to try it on came over me. Everything else—" she glanced around the room "—just sort of followed."

"It looks good on you." He moved to the third button and lifted his gaze to hers. "The white against your eyes deepens the blue."

Dylan barely heard Jessica's whispered thank-you. He leaned closer. "I've never met anyone like you, Jessica Stone," he said quietly.

Her eyelids were heavy as she held his gaze. "I'm not sure that's a compliment."

He smiled. "It's a compliment."

"Thank you."

When he got to the fourth button, he felt her breath catch. His knuckles brushed the swell of her breast through the lace. "I thought you were a ghost when I came in here. You're too beautiful to be real."

"I'm real," she murmured.

"I know. You're more real than any woman I've ever met. So real it frightens the hell out of me."

"I frighten you?" she asked in wonder.

He nodded slowly. "You make me want things, Jess. Things I can't have."

"It's Christmas Eve. Anything's possible if you believe." She lifted a hand to his cheek. "But you have to tell me what it is you want."

He felt her heart pounding under his hand, felt the answering beat of his own thundering heart. "You," he said softly. "I want you."

Jessica understood there were no promises, but for this one night, she refused to care. His skin felt warm under her hand, and the beginning of a beard tickled at her fingertips. She looked into his eyes, saw the urgency and need there, and felt as if she was looking into a mirror.

Candlelight surrounded them like a fiery cocoon. She sighed his name, leaning close, offering the most precious gift she could give him. A gift that could never be taken back once given. A gift, she knew, that would never be given to anyone else.

His lips brushed hers lightly, tracing the contours of her mouth before his tongue followed suit, tasting, testing. His hand cupped her breast and she arched into him, marveling at the magic his palm worked. He was gentle, so incredibly gentle, she thought she might cry.

She felt weightless, as if her body were drifting. She felt his lips move over her lips like a whisper, no more than the flutter of a butterfly's wings.

This was like nothing she'd ever experienced before or ever would again. Her hands slid around his neck, pulling him closer, then closer still, wanting to be a part of him, wanting him to be a part of her. There was desire, there was passion, but there was more, so much more.

What was happening? Dylan wondered. She was everything a man dreamed of, everything a man could want. It wasn't possible to feel this desperate, this out of control. It was as if he was on the outer edge of a branch, watching in helpless despair as the limb snapped in two. He felt himself fall and he held on to her, knowing she was his only salvation. His only chance.

The need for her sharpened and grew. He rained kisses on her mouth and neck. She molded herself to him, murmuring encouragement, whispering his name. He drew her away, his breathing ragged as he looked down at her, she up at him. Her irises were dilated, her lips swollen and wet from his kisses.

"Touch me," she whispered. "Please."

It was impossible to resist her. He couldn't. It would have been easier to stop the sun from rising. One by one, he slowly undid the front buttons of her dress, then carefully pushed the heavy fabric aside.

Her underclothes were as much a surprise to him as the dress. The cotton chemise dipped low, with one faded pink ribbon at the V of the demure garment. He tugged gently at the ribbon and the chemise fell open, exposing her breasts to him. His palms felt damp, his skin hot, as he stared down at her. "Beautiful," he murmured, and a blush rose on her cheeks.

He couldn't take his eyes off her as he slipped the chemise and dress completely from her shoulders. Her skin glowed like smooth porcelain. She trembled when he brought his lips to her shoulder. His hands slid around her rib cage, his knuckles brushing the velvety underside of her breasts. She gasped when his mouth covered one swollen nipple; she moaned as his tongue swirled hot and wet over the beaded tip.

Sensation after sensation exploded inside her. A need sharper and clearer than she'd ever felt before coiled low in her stomach. She was incapable of thought. She could only feel. And the feelings were so intense she thought she might rip apart from the force. She held him to her, burying her fingers in his hair as he lowered her to the floor. The pillow was soft under her head, the rug coarse against her back. She cupped his head in her hands, moaning as he wet one nipple with his tongue, then pulled the hardened peak into his mouth.

What had started with such tenderness became urgent and wild. She worked at the buttons of his shirt, needing to feel his skin against her own. She lifted her hips as he slid the dress and chemise down her body, then her hands fanned across his bare chest and tugged the shirt from him.

He pushed to his knees, rising over her, his eyes glinting with passion as he unbuckled his belt and slid his zipper down. Boldly he tugged off his jeans. Naked, he lowered himself, parting her legs with his muscular thighs.

He entered her, his gaze burning into hers. The pain of wanting, the pleasure, became one, and she grasped his arms, holding on to him as he filled her with maddening slowness. Impatient, she arched up to meet him, driving him deeply into her. His moan echoed her own, and as he rolled his hips, she laced her fingers around his neck, pulling him closer still, wishing she could draw herself inside him.

The candlelight circled them; their shadows rose and fell on the wall. The flames within them rose higher, then higher still, until the blaze overtook them and exploded, shattering into a thousand brilliant sparks.

And as the embers slowly settled, he held her close, listening to the sweet sound of her heartbeat.

"Is it not the most wonderful gift ever?" Meggie asked, her eyes bright as she spun in front of the altar. "We have

our church again, Lucas. Our beautiful church. How can we ever thank her?''

Lucas watched Meggie's skirts fly as she turned. She'd never looked so radiant. At least, not for a hundred and twenty years. He smiled, pleasured by her delight. ''We'll find a way, my love.''

''If only we knew who the nasty individual was who set the saloon on fire. We could expose the scoundrel somehow.''

Lucas shook his head. ''Since we didn't see, we can't know. Not even Hannibal saw who it was.'' Lucas looked at the dog, who had shown up a few minutes ago with news that Dylan had returned. There was no telepathy involved to understand that the hotel was off-limits tonight.

''We'll all have to be more watchful, then,'' Meggie declared. ''We can't let anything happen to Jessica or to Makeshift. Where would we go, what would we do, if it was gone?''

Lucas didn't know. Frustration boiled in him. There were so many things he didn't know. With every advantage he experienced as a spirit being came a limitation that sorely tested his patience.

But what worried him the most, what he hadn't even told Meggie, was the feeling that he was being drawn from her, away from Makeshift. He'd fought the sensation, but he understood that if it was finally time for him to leave here, there was nothing he could do to stop it.

He couldn't think about it. The idea of leaving Meggie here alone was inconceivable.

''Dance with me, Lucas,'' Meggie whispered. ''A Christmas dance.''

''I'd be honored, my lady.'' He held his arms out, pretending, as they had so many times before. Smiling, she moved into his arms, also pretending.

And as they glided over the floor, somewhere the pretense became reality, and for the first time in one hundred *and twenty years, Lucas held the woman he loved in his arms.*

Sunlight woke Jessica the next morning. Sunlight, and a wet sloppy kiss on her cheek. A little *too* wet and sloppy, she thought, slowly opening her eyes. Hannibal stared back from beside her bed, his tongue hanging sideways out of his jaws. She burrowed under her pillow, but the dog barked and nudged her with his cold nose.

"Go away," she moaned.

He waited a moment, then nudged her again.

"I said go away."

"That's not what you said last night," a deep voice whispered sensually as a large hand slid over the blanket covering her rear end.

Dylan. She smiled, then shivered as his touch grew more intimate. When the mattress dipped, she pulled her head out from under the pillow and combed her hair back from her face. Hannibal was gone, but Dylan sat on the edge of the bed, smiling down at her. They'd spent the night in her bed making love, and now, in the light of day, she felt the rise of a blush. Dylan wore jeans, but the snap was undone, and just looking at his bare muscular chest made her pulse leap.

"Really?" She feigned boredom. "I can't seem to remember."

He lifted one brow. "Is that right? Well, then, I'll just have to jog your memory."

His hand glided over the roundness of her buttocks and up her back. "Does this ring a bell?" he whispered.

An entire cathedral of bells, she thought as she drew in a sharp breath. It took every ounce of control she possessed to lie still while his hand moved upward. "It's still pretty blurry," she murmured.

"Maybe this will sharpen your focus." His teeth nibbled the back of her neck while his hand slid over the soft edge of her breast, then between her body and the mattress.

Razor sharp, was all she could think as he lowered his body beside hers. And when his hand moved lower and slipped between her legs, it was impossible not to squirm.

"It's coming back to me now." Wantonly she moved her hips against the delicious press of his fingers.

"Oh, it's coming all right," he said, chuckling softly as he rolled her onto her back and lowered his body over hers. She tugged at his zipper, then slid his jeans over his hips.

"Dylan!" she cried out as he slid into her.

"So your memory returns," he said raggedly, moving against her slowly.

"It's a miracle," she replied, wrapping her arms around him. "Truly a miracle."

"Merry Christmas." Dylan rose on his elbows and glanced down at Jessica. Her skin was flushed, her eyes heavy and dark from their lovemaking.

"Oh, my gosh." She squeezed her eyes shut. "I almost forgot!"

He pressed his lips to the pulse at the base of her neck. "Do you need another memory jog?"

She laughed softly, then gasped as his mouth traveled lower. "I've never forgotten Christmas, and besides, it's tradition in my family to get up and open presents with the first ray of light."

Her enthusiasm charmed him. He could picture her with dark-haired children surrounding her, excitedly opening stockings and presents on Christmas morning. When he unexpectedly saw himself standing beside her, he shook the image away. There was no place for him in fantasies like that.

"I've opened my present." He wiggled his brows at her and grinned.

She smiled, then ran her hands up his chest. "What did your parents do on Christmas when you were little?"

"They went to Europe," he said, rolling to his side and pulling her with him.

Her eyes widened. "You went to Europe every Christmas?"

"No. I said my parents did."

She stared at him for a long moment. "They left you at home?"

"They didn't leave me at home. They left me at boarding school. After they divorced, I sometimes went to stay at my mother's place on the Cape. She had a housekeeper named Gerta who loved to sing 'Yingle Bells.'"

Jessica ignored his attempt at humor. "Your mother left you with a housekeeper on *Christmas?*"

Her look of complete shock and sympathy almost made him smile. "Yeah, well, tradition, as you say. They'd been going to Europe every summer and December for years. Why let a little thing like a kid change their lives?"

Jessica felt her chest constrict. It was unthinkable not to be with family on Christmas. She knew hers would always be there for her—every day, not just Christmas. But obviously Dylan had never had that, and as she looked at him, she realized how little she knew about the man she loved.

She loved him. The thought nearly took the breath from her. She'd fought it from the first, but it had been there all the time, lying in wait. Yet no matter how much she wanted to tell him, she wouldn't. He would pull away from her, and she couldn't bear that. Not now. Not today.

She cupped his face in her hands and held his gaze with hers. "I'm sorry, Dylan," she said softly.

One corner of his mouth tilted upward. "Don't be sorry. You should've seen the presents I got."

"Something tells me those presents didn't mean spit to you," she said quietly.

He pulled her body snugly against his. "The red Lamborghini I got for my high school graduation was pretty nice."

She nearly choked. "Lamborghini?"

He smiled at her reaction. "My father handed me the keys, then told me to report for work at his company for the summer until I started at the college he'd chosen. I drove that damn car until it ran out of gas, left it, then hitchhiked to Colorado."

With a gasp, she sat upright. "You abandoned a *Lamborghini?*"

Dylan rested his head back against the pillows and enjoyed the view of Jessica's body. He frowned playfully as she quickly pulled the sheet up to cover herself. "The price of owning it was too high for me. For the first time in my life I knew what it felt like to be free. No conditions, no strings."

"And then you got married," she said carefully.

"Ah, yes. Kathleen. A temporary lapse of sanity at my father's sixtieth birthday party, one of my rare visits home. It didn't take long for both of us to realize it was a mistake. We argued constantly about my going to work for my father's importing business. She'd moved out by the end of the fourth month, but when she discovered she was pregnant, she tried to use the baby to get me to go to work for my dad. If she—" he hesitated "—they hadn't died, I just might have done it."

Jessica's eyes burned as she slipped into the warmth of Dylan's arms and held him close. "I'm so sorry," she said quietly. "She was such a fool. And your parents need a sound talking to, as well," she added.

He chuckled softly. His fingers traced a lazy circle on her shoulder. "Now that I'd like to see you do. My dad still asks me when I'm going to grow up and come home to work for him."

The very idea that the rugged muscular man holding her—the man who'd made love to her half the night—wasn't grown-up was almost laughable. He'd had parents who expected too much, who tried to buy love with money, and a wife who'd tried to buy money with love. Dylan not only wasn't going home, Jessica realized with a heavy heart, he had no intention of making his own home, either. It was easier to drift, to move from place to place, than risk that kind of hurt again.

But today was Christmas, she thought. And no matter what tomorrow might bring, she was going to show Dylan a good old-fashioned Stone-family holiday.

Just as soon as he stopped kissing her neck.

There was a small spot just behind Jessica's ear that he knew was sensitive. He searched for it, and when she moaned, he smiled with satisfaction, much happier with the current conversation, or lack of it, which had nothing to do with family. He hadn't wanted to even think about family, let alone talk about it.

He wanted to regret last night, but he couldn't. The morning hadn't diminished his need for her, and even now, as the heat coiled inside him, he feared there would never be enough mornings to forget last night, or to forget her.

Jake and Jared would be coming over later for dinner. And after he talked to them, he knew he'd have to tell Jessica the truth.

But not today, he decided. He wouldn't do that to her on Christmas. Tomorrow morning. He'd talk to her then. If she was going to hate him, he didn't want it to be today.

"Is that popcorn *real?*"

Jessica handed a glass of wine to Myrna, then answered her question with a patience that could only be borne on Christmas. "Of course it's real. So are the cookies. That's why the bottom is so bare. Hannibal's been snacking." The dog wagged his tail at the sound of his name.

Jake and Jared stood beside Myrna surveying their sister's handiwork. "Good idea, Hannibal," Jake said, and snatched a star off one branch.

"Hey!" She tried to grab the cookie back.

"Edible ornaments." Jared stared hard at the tree, then settled for a bell cookie. "Sort of like a giant appetizer plate."

"Aunt Savannah! Annie!" Emma yelled for reinforcements from the kitchen. "Jake and Jared are eating Jessie's tree!"

Savannah came out of the kitchen carrying a platter with a huge golden brown turkey. "Well, I guess we better feed them, then, before they start on the furniture."

Annie's arms were equally laden with bowls of mashed potatoes and gravy. She followed Savannah into the dining room. "I hate to admit it, but that tree looked good enough to eat to me, too."

"Everything looks good to you lately." Jared went into the dining room and took the bowls from Annie's hands, then slipped one arm around her waist and covered her belly with his hand.

It was strange being included in the festivities, Dylan thought as they all sat for dinner and the blessing was said. Yet at the same time, he felt at home here, welcomed in a way he'd never experienced before. They'd treated him as one of the family, not as a guest, and his duties for the day had included peeling potatoes and cutting up bread for stuffing.

He'd tried several times to catch Jared and Jake long enough to talk privately with them, but there'd been too much commotion. He'd just have to wait until the time was right. As if the time would ever be right to hurt Jessica, he thought miserably. Her brilliant smile lit the room as she kissed and hugged each member of her family, including Myrna and Carlton, and wished them a Merry Christmas. The sound of Christmas songs filled the house, and the delicious smell of food cooking permeated the air.

There were toasts at dinner. Silly toasts, insulting toasts, heartfelt toasts. Jessica sat at the opposite end of the table,

laughing and eating, teasing and talking. He wanted to remember her like this, every detail, no matter how small.

"So, Dylan—" Carlton interrupted his thoughts
"—how's the project coming along?"

"Fine." Dylan forced his attention to the elderly man,
thinking he looked paler than he had earlier. "Other than a
short in the wiring I still haven't found, the church is finished. So is part of the hotel."

Jessica handed a nearly empty bowl of stuffing to Jared.
"You have to see Dylan's blueprints. They're wonderful."

"There's talk in town the city might revoke your permits, dear," Myrna said, waving her fork. "There's been
some complaints about minors working out here."

Even on Christmas patience had its limits, Jessica thought
with a sigh. She'd known it had been too much to hope for
when the day had nearly passed and Myrna hadn't started
in once.

Determined not to let Myrna get another word in, Jessica quickly said, "By the way, I'm taking everyone to the
church after dinner. I thought we'd light some candles and
sing carols."

Remembering the candlelight they'd made love to the
night before, Jessica glanced at Dylan. She felt her heart
skip a beat at the dark intensity that shone in his eyes as he
held her gaze.

"Oh, Jessica, what a beautiful idea!" Annie said, then
looked at Jared. "We should have waited and been married
there."

Jared leaned over and kissed his wife. "I waited four
years for you. I wasn't waiting one more day."

"That leaves you, Jessica," Jake said. "Anybody you'd
like us to round up and herd in for you?"

Jessica half expected Dylan to bolt from the room at
Jake's comment. To her surprise, he didn't look away. If
anything, his gaze only grew more intense. "I'll do my own

herding, thank you very much," she said coolly, drawing her attention back to her brother.

"Hey, don't forget about me," Emma said indignantly. "I wanna get married, too."

They all laughed then, and the dishes were soon gathered up. While everyone else piled into the kitchen, Carlton excused himself and went upstairs to rest. Myrna complained the doctors had overmedicated him, which was why he moved so slowly, but Jessica suspected there was a problem much greater than Myrna was willing to face. Jessica also knew that Carlton's illness embarrassed the man. He'd been a high-powered in-control executive his entire life. A man who'd raised his only daughter alone, showering her with gifts. He'd given her everything but himself.

Like Dylan's parents, she thought sadly, drying the last dish and putting it in the cupboard.

Jessica glanced at her brothers and Dylan. Their heads were bowed intently over the kitchen table; they were discussing the "easy" instructions for assembling an outdoor playhouse for Emma. A warmth spread through her at the sight of Dylan conversing so easily with her family. But then, she felt warm every time she looked at Dylan, or even thought about him, for that matter.

"Jess, can we go see the church now?" Emma asked.

"Sure, sweetie." Jessica hugged her younger sister. She'd come to the Stone family late in their lives, but they loved her as if she'd been there from the first.

"You boys 'bout ready?" Jessica asked.

Dylan glanced up from the table and saw the loving exchange between Jessica and Emma. That was how she'd be with her own children, he knew. Gentle and loving. He'd missed that in his life, but he never knew how much until today.

Some things a person was better off not knowing. He'd never again be able to think of Christmas or candles—or even cookies—without seeing her face and remembering how it had felt to hold her in his arms.

But he knew what he had to do, and it could be put off no longer.

"I thought I'd take a minute and show Jake and Jared the blueprints," Dylan said, glancing at Jared.

Jared nodded in understanding. "You go ahead, sis. We'll be along in a minute."

With a grin, she tossed a towel onto the counter. "All right, but you're all in big trouble if I have to come back here for you." Savannah and Annie seconded Jessica's statement, then they all headed for the church with Myrna fussing about how difficult it was to walk in the dirt with high heels.

Dylan watched from the kitchen window until the women were out of sight, then explained about the fire in the saloon and his suspicions about its origin.

"It's sounding too familiar," Jake said with a frown. "I lost my barn in a fire a few months back, then Jared's office blew up. They weren't accidents, and something tells me this isn't, either."

"What about those kids?" Jared asked. "You think one of them might've done it?"

Dylan shook his head. "I don't want to believe that, but I'm not ruling out anyone yet."

"That does it, then," Jake said firmly. "That girl is going back to town. She's not safe here."

"I already tried that argument." Dylan leaned against the counter. "She wouldn't have any part of it."

"That girl is too damn stubborn for her own good," Jared said with annoyance. "Thank God I talked you into coming here and keeping an eye on her. I don't know what we'd do without you, pal."

"That's what I have to talk to you about." Dylan sighed and dragged his hands through his hair. "I can't keep lying to Jessica. I'm going to tell her the truth in the morning."

"I think I'd rather hear it now."

Dylan froze, then turned slowly at the sound of the too-familiar voice. She stood in the doorway, her eyes burning into his as she waited for his answer.

Eleven

"I needed matches," she said and moved slowly into the room, never taking her eyes off Dylan. His expression was rigid, his jaw like granite as he watched her approach.

Jared was the first to move. "Jess, let me explain—"

"I want Dylan to explain," she said flatly. "Every little detail, Mr. Grant, starting with how you know my brothers."

A muscle jumped in Dylan's temple. He never let go of her gaze. "Jared and I met in South America on an oil project where I was the structural engineer."

South America. She should have known. It had been right in front of her all the time. *Idiot.* She was such a fool.

Pride held her chin up and kept her legs from folding under her as she stood in front of Dylan. She wouldn't let him see her pain. He didn't deserve to see it. "South America is hardly the next block. You must be pretty good friends for you to come all the way to the States and baby-sit me."

Jake rose from his chair. "Jessie, it wasn't—"

"Be quiet, Jake," Jessica said quietly, and the cold precision of her words stopped him. He sat back down and sighed. She folded her arms. "Go on, Dylan."

Dylan's mouth thinned. "Jared and Jake were worried about you. They didn't think it was safe for you out here alone."

"So Jared called you," she said, her voice dripping with sarcasm. "A big strong trustworthy man. Someone they could count on to keep an eye on me and file weekly reports. I'd love to know what you included in those reports, Mr. Grant. I'm sure they'd be fascinating reading."

His eyes darkened with anger, but she didn't care. She was quickly shifting from a state of numbness to slow-burning fury.

"My God, this is so funny." She forced a dry laugh. "Jared's performance when I introduced you was worthy of an Academy Award. And Jake inviting you to his house, pretending to interrogate you because he *cared* about me. And you, Dylan, all that nonsense about room and board when you knew you'd take the job, anyway."

"Jessie," Jared said, "don't be mad at Dylan. He was just doing me a favor."

"A favor?" Her eyes sharpened as she stared furiously at her brothers. "Making a fool of me, interfering in my life, *lying* to me, that's a *favor?*"

Jared stared at the floor, while Jake twirled his Stetson in his hand. Neither one would look at her. Except for Dylan. His gaze nearly burned a hole through her.

She put her hands on her hips and moved closer to him. "And wasn't it a hoot when I accused you of being afraid of my brothers?"

Jared glanced up. "Why would you accuse him of that?"

She smiled. "Yes, Dylan. Why would I?"

His eyes narrowed. "Jessica," he said tightly, "let me talk to you alone."

"Alone?" She threw her arms out. "Whyever would we need to be alone? Surely anything you have to say you can say in front of my brothers. There're no secrets between you guys."

Dylan had known this was going to be difficult, but he'd never even come close to realizing *how* difficult. In spite of Jessica's cool demeanor, he saw the hurt in her eyes, the anger. He didn't blame her. She'd told him once how much she hated lies, and now she'd caught him sitting smack-dab in the middle of one.

He shot a look at Jared, who nodded in understanding, then stood and faced his sister. "Jess, we can talk later and sort through this. Jake and I will go on down to the church. You and Dylan can join us after you've chewed this for a while."

She opened her mouth to argue, then shut it again.

Jake jammed his hat on his head, hesitated, then shuffled out the back door when Jessica glared at him. Jared cast one long worried look at Dylan, then sighed deeply and followed his brother.

When she turned back to him with her arms folded protectively in front of her, Dylan felt his insides twist. He watched her square her shoulders and look him in the eye.

"I trusted you," she said without emotion.

"I know. I'm sorry."

"You lied to me."

"Yes."

"Stop agreeing with me, dammit!"

She swung around, pacing away, then back again. "I asked myself why a man with your qualifications would want a job for such low pay. I even questioned your little slipup when you mentioned Venezuela. But what should really have tipped me off was the fact that Jared and Jake weren't coming around here like I'd expected. They didn't need to. They already had an undercover agent doing their dirty work. I doubt they know exactly *how* undercover you got, do they?''

His control slipped. He grabbed her by the shoulders and forced her to look at him. "What happened between you and me is nobody's business but ours. It has nothing to do with your brothers."

"It's just so hysterical." She tried to pull away, but he held her tight. "I mean, your coming here to protect me, and you end up in my bed. 'Course, there was protection there, too, so you really have nothing to feel guilty about, Dylan. You did your job."

"Dammit, Jessica. Don't minimize or make light of our making love."

Anger ruled her words now. Anger and hurt. She might regret them later, but there was so much she'd regret, what was one more thing? "Is that what you call it? Making love?" She stared defiantly at him. "There are other expressions more appropriate, you know."

His hands tightened painfully on her shoulders. "Stop it. You're special to me. You know that. You have to know that."

"I don't know anything," she said. "Like how you could do this to me."

"Jessica—" he softened his hold "—I never meant to hurt you. I tried my damnedest to keep my hands off you."

"That's what all that guilt was about," she said, wondering how she could stand here and face him when her heart was shattering into a thousand pieces. "Breaking my brothers' trust. It had nothing to do with caring about me."

He pulled her closer. "That's not true. You know it's not."

She hated the moisture she felt burn her eyes. But not as much as she hated the reaction her body still had to his closeness. *A lie. Everything had been one big lie.* "Why couldn't you have been honest before things went too far?"

"And what would you have done if I'd told you?"

"Exactly what I'm going to do now." She pulled out of his grasp, then lifted her chin and looked him in the eyes. "You're fired."

His eyes narrowed. "What about Makeshift? You can't let the project fall apart because I lied to you."

She was the only thing falling apart at the moment. But she wouldn't let him know that. "The church is finished, and enough of the hotel is done for the review committee to get a clear picture of what I want to do here. We'll proceed as before, as soon as I find another foreman to take your place." She'd intended her words to be a verbal blow, and from the murderous expression on Dylan's face, she'd succeeded. Strange, she thought, but she felt no satisfaction, only an empty black feeling inside her chest.

He started to move toward her again, but she put up a hand and stepped back. "I mean it, Dylan. I can't work with someone I don't trust. I'm going to join my family now, and I'd appreciate it if you were gone by the time I got back."

His eyes were like black ice as he stared at her, then he turned and stalked out of the room. She blinked, refusing to give in to tears now. Everyone was waiting for her at the church, and she still needed what strength she could muster to face her brothers. She'd have the time and the privacy later to give in to the pain slicing through her.

She drew a slow fortifying breath and swallowed hard. It was Christmas, after all. The most special day of the year.

"How could you—either of you—do such a thing?"

Savannah stood over Jake, her eyes narrowed as she frowned at her husband. Holding the same posture, Annie stood over Jared. The men shifted uncomfortably in the church pew, their expressions repentant. Jessica sat in the pew in front of them, refusing even to look at her siblings.

"She's twenty-seven years old," Savannah said. "An intelligent, responsible, resourceful woman who is capable of handling her own affairs."

Jessica flinched at Savannah's choice of words, but kept her back stiffly to her brothers. The candles on the altar had been lit, and the room glowed with a warm soft light. The fingers she'd laced in her lap were ice-cold.

At least she'd managed to get rid of Myrna before the fireworks had begun, Jessica thought. She'd asked her stepmother to go back for more candles and to check on Carlton. Emma needed to use the bathroom and had gone along.

"It was for Jessie's own good," Jared protested. "You both know what happened to Jake and me. Someone out there wants Stone Creek and is willing to do anything to get it."

"Nobody likes to be lied to," Savannah said. "I seem to recall a misunderstanding at our first meeting. You were furious I lied about being Emma's mother, instead of her aunt."

"This is different." Jake folded his arms.

"Different?" Jessica had been quiet long enough. She turned and faced her brothers. "How like a man to arrange the rules to suit himself," she said angrily. "A favor, I believe you called it. One friend doing a good deed for another."

"He *is* a friend," Jared declared.

"And I'm just your sister, right?" she said quietly.

Both Jake and Jared stared at their feet.

Jessica felt as if she were being turned inside out. She'd thought that Dylan cared for her, she'd even hoped that . . .

She squeezed her eyes shut. It didn't matter now what she'd hoped.

"Look, Jess," Jake said, "let's all go back to the hotel and straighten this out. You know the truth now and there's no harm done. Just talk to Dylan."

No harm done? A bubble of hysteria threatened to burst inside her. No harm done? She'd fallen in love with a lie, and the betrayal was like a knife in her heart.

"There's nothing to go back and talk about," she said, suddenly exhausted. "I fired him and asked him to leave."

Jared shook his head. "Aw, Jess, you can't—"

She cut him off with a wave of her hand. "Don't tell me what I can't, Jared Stone. Any foreman should be able to read Dylan's blueprints. I'm going to put an ad in the paper tomorrow and find another man right away."

Even as she said the words she felt the ache in her chest sharpen. There'd never be another man like Dylan.

"Jess," Jared said softly, and leaned closer to his sister. "Please don't be mad. Jake and I couldn't let you come out here by yourself. What if something happened to you? How would we get along without you?"

His words were spoken with such tenderness, such sincerity, that Jessica's anger eased. She couldn't imagine anything happening to one of them, either. She'd been through that pain after Jonathan's and her parents' deaths. The thought of ever going through that again was more than she could bear.

"We love you, Jessie," Jake said, coming closer. "I'm sorry if we hurt you."

They were her brothers. They would always be there for her, as she would always be there for them. No matter what.

A tear slipped down her cheek. She sighed heavily, then slowly reached her hands out to them. Jared took one hand, Jake the other. "I love you, too," she said softly. "I don't forgive either one of you yet, but I do love you."

And as she listened to the sound of Dylan's motorcycle tear out of town, her heart tightened painfully and she silently said goodbye.

"Don't cry, Meggie," Lucas said gently. "He'll be back."

Meggie's shoulders trembled as she held her hands to her face. "Oh, Lucas, how could he leave like that?"

"Well, she did throw him out," Lucas said.

Meggie looked up indignantly. "But she loves him. Why doesn't he understand that?"

Lucas thought it best not to explain that men rarely understood women. "Perhaps a little time will help clear his mind, and Jessica's, too. She was a little emotional tonight."

"She was not," Meggie defended Jessica. "She's hurt, that's all. If he had told her sooner, instead of her finding out that way, she never would have told him to leave."

"Perhaps." When it came to women, speculation was a dangerous thing. "We shall see."

"What if he doesn't come back?" Meggie asked. "What will happen to Jessica and Makeshift? What will happen to us?"

He'd had the same concern. Since Dylan had left, both he and Meggie had dimmed, and the tactile ability they'd developed had disappeared. "We'll be fine, my love," he reassured her. "We've been here for one hundred and twenty years. Nothing is going to change now."

But even as he spoke the words, Lucas knew they weren't true. Something was changing. It was almost as if a huge magnet were pulling him in another direction, and he was being drawn away from Meggie. Since Dylan had left, the pull had intensified twofold. He knew that it was nearly time, and that he'd be leaving Makeshift soon.

And the thought of leaving here, without Meggie, terrified him beyond words.

"Thank you, Mr. Green." Jessica smiled stiffly at the pale reed-thin man sitting across from her in the Bronco Diner. "I'll give you a call as soon as I've made my decision."

The man's Adam's apple bobbed as he grinned and shook her hand vigorously, nearly rattling her teeth. She sighed heavily when he left, then sank back into the booth. Her fourth applicant that morning, and still no luck.

What did she expect? Every man that walked in here she compared to Dylan.

I'm hiring the next man that sits across from me, she vowed. She didn't care if he couldn't put Lincoln logs together. She couldn't keep going through this.

She glanced at her appointment schedule. Her next applicant was due in ten minutes. A Mr. Conrad Trite. If the man could pick up a hammer and knew which end to use, she'd hire him.

Three days had passed since Christmas. The kids had been able to work without Dylan for the short term, anyway, but she knew they needed experienced supervision. There'd been a marked change in their enthusiasm, though. Especially Dean's. His chin had been dragging the ground ever since he heard that Dylan was gone. But then, she certainly hadn't fared well, herself.

He'd left three messages on her machine, but she hadn't called him back. She assumed he'd left town by now. There was no reason for him to stay, was there?

What a fool she'd been. Her pride would heal, she knew, but her heart was a different story. She felt as if there was an emptiness inside her, a bottomless black hole that could never be filled.

The smell of grilled food made her stomach growl, and she realized it was lunchtime. She reached for the menu when Susan set a plate filled with french fries and a hamburger on the table.

Jessica glanced at the waitress. "I didn't order this."

She refilled Jessica's coffee and nodded to the corner booth by the front door. "He did."

Frowning, Jessica looked over her shoulder.

Dylan.

Her heart started to pound as their gazes locked. Her first impulse was to jump over the table and throw herself on his lap. The second was to dump the plate of food over his head.

She turned quickly around, determined not to let him see her in such a vulnerable state.

When he slid into her booth across from her, she studied the information she'd taken on each of the applicants. She wanted to pick up her pen, but her fingers were shaking too much.

"Hi."

She said nothing, just continued to read through her notes.

"I'm here for my appointment," he said.

She glanced up sharply at him.

"Mr. Conrad Trite." He pointed at the list. "You know, Con Trite." He leaned closer. "As in, I'm sorry."

She bit her lip to keep from smiling. Now that she thought about it, the man *had* sounded strange on the phone, as if he'd just swallowed a chicken bone.

She straightened her back and placed her forearms on the table. "I'm afraid the position is not open to you, because apologies are like your name—trite."

He looked tired, she thought. Wonderfully, beautifully tired. A little rumpled, as if he'd just woken up. She remembered what it felt like to wake up beside him, feel his hands on her skin, on her—

Stop. She couldn't let herself think about him. Not now. Not ever.

"How are you?" he asked quietly.

"I'm fine," she lied. She didn't ask how he was.

"How's my crew doing?"

His sincere concern for the kids put a chink in her armor, but she ignored it. "*My* crew is doing well, thank you. They'll be able to keep going on the projects you gave each of them for a few days. I'll have a foreman hired by the time they're ready to start something new."

"Any luck with your applicants?" He pointed at her list.

"I'll find someone. Life, I assure you, does go on."

He reached across the table and took her hands. "Jessica, stop it," he said sharply, keeping his voice down. "This isn't like you."

"Isn't like me?" She tried to pull her hands away, but he held her tight. Unless she wanted to make a scene, she was trapped. "Mister, don't flatter yourself that you know me so well."

His thumbs moved over the backs of her hands. "I know you're the most honest, most beautiful woman I've ever met. You see the good in people—you believe in people. It's a rare quality. And the thought of hurting you, of destroying that rare quality, sickens me."

His thumbs, with their rough texture, moving over her skin sent electricity shooting up her arms. She wouldn't weaken now. She couldn't. Her anger was the only thing that held her together. "The Stones don't destroy so easily, Dylan. I wouldn't give it another thought."

"Dammit, Jess." He leaned across the table. "I'm sorry. What else can I say?"

That you love me. Even as she thought it, she hated herself for being so weak. For still holding on to glass hopes and wishes made of sand.

She didn't want to fight anymore. She didn't have the strength or energy. "Is that what you want from me? To accept your apology? All right—" she stared straight into his eyes "—apology accepted. You can walk out of here now, conscience clear, Mr. Grant. Go back to South America or one of the other dozens of places you've been running to your entire life. I'm going to be fine."

A muscle worked in Dylan's jaw. He released her hands, then slid out of the booth and stared down at her. "Whatever you think of me, Jess, however you remember me, I want you to know I never meant to hurt you."

She looked up at him, and the need to feel his arms around her grew with painful intensity. Her chest tightened, her throat felt thick. Between heartbeats, she thought for one wild moment that she'd take whatever he might offer, even one night. Even one afternoon.

But she'd let her heart rule her head with Dylan before. She couldn't do it again. No matter what she'd told him about Stone determination, she wasn't sure she could survive another goodbye.

"Hey, Jess."

Jessica turned. Sam had just come in the front door of the diner. A mixture of frustration and relief poured through her as he moved toward her. She felt Dylan tense beside her.

Sam touched the brim of his cowboy hat to Dylan. "Hey, Dylan."

Dylan nodded stiffly.

"Dylan was just leaving." Jessica forced a smile and gestured to the seat across from her. "Why don't you take his place?"

Anger tightened Dylan's expression. His eyes narrowed dangerously, and the look he shot her was like a torch to her insides. "Goodbye, Dylan," she said quietly.

He left without a word, rattling the glass door of the diner as he slammed it behind him. The waitress looked up with a frown, and Sam lifted his brows.

"It's a long story," she said with a sigh, staring at the cold hamburger and fries. Her stomach rolled.

He pointed to the plate. "You gonna eat this?"

She shook her head and he dug in. Food never went to waste around a hardworking rancher.

Without giving details, Jessica told Sam what Jake and Jared had done. He tried to be the diplomat, but she sensed he sided with Jared and Jake. Sam was like a big brother to her, though she realized that their relationship could shift if she encouraged any change. But she knew she'd never think of Sam as more than a friend. After Dylan, she might never think of any man as more than a friend.

* * *

It was dark by the time she got back to Makeshift. She'd finished the day with ten interviews, none of them promising, but she was determined to choose one and at least give him a try.

She stepped out of her truck, listening to the bark of a coyote and the call of a bird. The night was cool, and the scent of mesquite filled the air.

It had never felt lonely here before Dylan. She'd always felt the presence of Meggie and Lucas, and Hannibal was always there to talk to, even though the conversation was one-sided.

Where was Hannibal? She glanced around. She'd told the kids after they finished for the day to leave the dog outside.

A full moon lit the streets, but the shadows were dark and, for the first time, a little frightening.

"Hannibal!"

She called him several times, but there was no answering bark. He'd always greeted her immediately when she came back from town.

Fear began to creep along her spine. She walked through the town, whistling for him, moving toward the church. Her heart pounded harder as every minute passed with no answer.

A soft light wavered from inside the church. Jessica froze. No one should be here. Quietly she opened the side door and slipped inside, pressing herself against the wall. A single candle burned on the altar. She started to move forward when she suddenly tripped over something at her feet. Something large and furry.

"Hannibal!"

Twelve

He needed to hit something. Smash something. He needed to release the devil inside him and howl his rage at the moon slowly moving up into the sky.

Fists clenched, Dylan paced his hotel room. She was the most infuriating woman he'd ever met. The most stubborn, foolhardy, unreasonable—

A knock at the door curtailed his list.

"What!" He threw open the door.

It was Dean. The teenager stared at Dylan, saw the anger on his face, then backed away. "Sorry. Guess I caught you at a bad time."

Dylan felt like an idiot. Dean had seen enough anger in his life. He didn't need it from him, as well. "No." He dragged a hand through his hair and stepped back. "Come on in. It's fine."

Dean hesitated, then shoved his hands into his pockets and moved inside. "I heard you were leaving."

Dylan knew the teenager had heard more than that. It was no longer a secret why he'd come here. He nodded, closing the door. " 'Fraid so."

"I also heard Jessica was hiring someone else."

Someone to take my place. He could still plainly see her sitting with Sam when he'd left her earlier. Anger threatened to erupt again and he quickly reined it in. "She's going to need a good foreman."

"You were a good foreman."

Dylan looked at the young man and realized that Dean didn't want him to leave. Dylan couldn't remember anyone particularly caring if he stayed or left.

A heaviness came over him, centering in his chest. "I can't stay," he said. "My coming here was wrong. My intentions may have been good, but the fact is, I lied. By helping Jared, I only ended up hurting Jessica. She deserved better than that."

She deserved a hell of a lot more, Dylan thought. Candles and flowers and diamond rings. Things he knew nothing about. Things that scared the hell out of him.

"She left town a few minutes ago," Dean said. "I thought that maybe, well, you know, you patched things up."

Dylan shook his head.

"Can't you just say you're sorry?"

Dylan sighed, then gestured for Dean to sit at the table in the corner. "I tried. She didn't go for it."

Dean settled on the edge of a chair and glanced down at the hands he'd dropped between his legs. "Maybe you could try harder."

"Dean," Dylan said quietly, "even if she did accept my apology, I still can't stay. It wouldn't be right now."

He could hardly tell the teenager that he couldn't stay because if he did he'd want Jessica every second of every day, and the wanting would make him crazy. It was better this way. He'd still want her, he'd still think about her, but he wouldn't hurt her any more than he already had.

Shoulders stiff, Dean straightened and looked Dylan in the eye. "Take me with you. Me and Troy."

Stunned, Dylan simply stared at the young man. He'd been caught completely off guard. Dean's eyes were bright with determination, his mouth set.

"I'll be eighteen next month. My dad's drinking so much lately he probably wouldn't notice we were gone for weeks. Not that he would care if he did notice."

"Dean, I . . . I can't do that. Troy is only nine. You can't take him away."

"I can and I will," he said fiercely, then added more softly, "We won't be any trouble. You said yourself I'm a good carpenter. I'll find work and pay our way."

Dylan didn't know what to say. He'd traveled alone for years. The idea of hauling a teenager and a nine-year-old around the country or through the jungles of South America was inconceivable.

"I can't, Dean," Dylan said as gently as possible. "My life is no way for you or Troy to live. Hell, it's no way for even me to live. I couldn't do that to either one of you."

A cold blank look came over Dean. He rose slowly and stuck out his hand. "Yeah, well, thanks, anyway."

Dammit, why can't I think of the right thing to say? Dylan thought. Why didn't he know what to do? He couldn't stand the look of hopelessness in Dean's eyes.

"Dean, Jessica needs you here," Dylan said finally. "When that center of hers is up and running in a few months, maybe you and Troy can live there, at least until your dad gets straightened out."

"Yeah, I'm sure you're right. It was a pretty crazy idea, anyhow. I'll be okay." He smiled tightly. "Well, see you around sometime."

Dylan didn't believe for a second that Dean was okay. And to a kid in trouble, a few months was an eternity. Dylan watched the teenager leave, quietly closing the door behind him.

With an oath, Dylan started to throw his things into his duffel bag. He'd done enough damage here. It was time to get the hell out.

When he picked up the gloves Jessica had given him Christmas Eve, he stopped and stared at them. A dull ache spread through his chest as he fingered the smooth leather. Without thinking, he slipped them on and curled his fingers tightly as he tested the feel.

A perfect fit.

He could still see the smile in her eyes as she'd handed him the present. A gift from the heart. Everything Jessica did, everything she gave, was from the heart.

A knot tightened in his stomach. She'd not only trusted him, she'd given him the most precious gift a woman could give a man, and he'd betrayed that trust.

She loved him. He knew that, though he'd never given her an opportunity to say it. He'd kept her at a distance, held himself back, not physically, of course, but emotionally. He'd never believed the kind of love Jessica offered him truly existed. All he had to do was accept that love, believe in it, and it was his.

The thought scared the hell out of him. He'd spent a lifetime avoiding commitment, of not allowing anything or anyone to control him. Was it possible to let go of that safety net now?

But the answer wasn't here, he realized as he stared at his hands. It was back at Makeshift. With Jessica.

Jessica dropped to her knees. "Hannibal!"

He didn't move, though she called his name several times. Panic overwhelmed her. She ran her hands over his still body, digging her fingers into his fur to see if he'd been hurt. He had to be all right. *He had to be!*

Holding back a sob, she laid her head on his chest. It was warm. She listened carefully, holding her breath. A heartbeat. It was there. Faint, perhaps, but at least it was there.

She jerked her head up at the sound of a cough from the shadows on the other side of the doorway. "Who's there?"

There was a movement from the darkness, then the silhouette of a man. It was impossible to make out his features.

Breath held, Jessica watched as the man moved forward slowly, until the light of the candle burning on the altar reflected off his face.

Carlton.

"What did you do to Hannibal?" she asked desperately.

"Just a few tranquilizers in a nice hamburger. He found me in here tonight, I'm afraid, and seemed determined to prevent me from doing what I need to do."

She stood slowly. "What is it you need to do, Carlton?" she asked carefully.

He sighed. "You weren't supposed to find me, Jessica. I only needed another minute, then you'd never know I was here."

A chill ran up her spine at the distant sound of his voice. "Why are you here?"

He glanced around. "You've done a beautiful job rebuilding the church. The review board would have been impressed."

She fought back her rising fear. "What do you mean, 'would have been impressed'?"

"It's too bad there was a short in the church," Carlton said. "They're dangerous, you know. Fires start that way all the time."

Fire? Jessica's heart stopped, then raced at Carlton's words. *Keep him talking,* she told herself. Anything to buy a little time so she could think, try to understand why he was doing this. "It was you, wasn't it?" she asked, struggling to keep the panic out of her voice. "All this time, you were the one who's been trying to force my brothers and me off Stone Creek. How could you hurt us like that?"

His skin was nearly white in the candlelight, his eyes sunken. "Both of the young men I hired to make problems for Jake and Jared had specific instructions that no one was to be hurt."

"But people *were* hurt," she said tightly. "Savannah and Emma almost died in the barn fire, and Jared was nearly killed when his compressor blew up."

Carlton's face twisted with anger, and the glow from the candle created a frightening mask. "Those men were incompetent. Idiots."

Though she hated to leave Hannibal's side, Jessica moved toward Carlton. "Yeah. It's impossible to find good help these days, isn't it?"

"Precisely." He nodded his agreement, completely missing the sarcasm. "So with you, I decided to handle business myself. It's easy to stop a few shipments or lose an order."

"That was you?" She stared at him in disbelief. "How?"

"You're so naive, my dear. Money, of course. I have a great deal of it. Grease a few palms, as they so coarsely say, and anything is possible."

"And the fire in the saloon?"

"Yes, my dear. I'm afraid so."

Even faced with the truth, she couldn't believe it. Myrna's father had always used his money to get what he wanted, but she'd never known him to be mean. "How could you do this? We're family."

He shook his head. "Myrna's my only family. After her mother ran away with another man, I made a vow that my little girl would have everything she ever wanted. I kept that vow, too. Until your father died and left her with no land. Stone Creek was the one thing I couldn't buy her. You were all too damn stubborn to sell."

He started to cough then, a deep exhausting cough that left him gasping for air.

"Myrna doesn't know about this, does she?" Jessica asked when he'd composed himself again. "What will she say? Will she want land you cheated from us?"

Her question obviously distressed him. He pulled a handkerchief out of the pocket of the blue sports coat he wore and wiped at his brow. "She's not going to find out."

"I'm going to tell her, Carlton. I have to."

There was fear in his glazed eyes, something that Jessica had never seen before. He slipped his handkerchief back into his pocket, then reached behind him and locked the side door of the church. He threw the key into the darkness, and she heard it land somewhere with a metallic clink. "You can't do that, Jessica. I won't let you."

She looked to the front doors of the church and gauged the distance. She could outrun him and get back to her truck.

"I already locked those doors, too," he said calmly.

She still couldn't believe he would actually hurt her, but she realized he wasn't the same man she'd known all these years. "Carlton," she said softly, "you're sick. Let's go back to the hotel and talk."

"I'm dying, you know." He moved closer to the altar and stared at the candle's flame. "Myrna thinks it's just a little case of stress and overwork. But I only have a few weeks left."

"Then spend it with Myrna. Stop trying to buy her things. Give her yourself for whatever time you have left."

He shook his head slowly and picked up the candle. The flame wavered, sending grotesque shadows over his face. "This is the last thing I can do for her. The last thing I can give her. I'm sorry you found me here, Jessica. I truly am fond of you."

He pulled a plastic bag out of his pocket. When he opened the bag and pulled out a rag, Jessica smelled gasoline.

Oh, God, no! He was going to set the church on fire!

She forced herself to remain calm, but her insides were shaking. "Don't do this. Please. I'll sell you my land, Carlton. All of it."

He hesitated for a moment, then narrowed his eyes. "You're a terrible liar, my dear, but I commend the effort. I also want to thank you for firing Dylan. It was terribly difficult to get around the man when he was here, and my time was quickly running out."

She reached toward him as he lifted the candle to the rag. "No! Carlton. *Please,* no!"

"*Nooooo...*"

Another cry echoed Jessica's. The hollow desperate cry of a woman. It filled the church with its anguish. Carlton paused, confused at the unseen voice. A cold breeze lifted the ends of Jessica's hair, swirled around her, then circled Carlton.

The candle went out and they were in darkness.

The smell of sulfur lingered in the heavy air. Jessica couldn't see Carlton, but knew he was close. She heard the strike of a match, but there was no flame. Blindly she stumbled toward the man, determined to do whatever necessary to stop him.

A furious pounding from the front of the church made her scream.

"Jessica! Open the door!"

Dylan! It was Dylan! Relief poured through her as she turned and felt her way along the pews. "I can't. They're locked," she yelled.

He continued to pound, yelling her name. She was almost to the front of the church when a cold hand—Carlton's—wrapped around her arm and dragged her to the floor. She hit her head on the corner of a pew and white spots swam before her eyes.

Carlton lit another match. The flame burst to life, casting eerie shadows over everything. He lifted the match to the rag.

The front doors of the church flew open. Dylan rushed in, then froze at the sight of Carlton with the rag and the lit match.

"You're too late, Mr. Grant," Carlton said, bringing the match to the rag. "Too late."

It was no breeze this time, but a strong wind that blew through the church. Cold and furious, it swept over them, pulling the rag from Carlton's hand and nearly pushing Dylan back. The match went out again, and a woman's cry was distinctly heard over the roar of the wind.

They were in darkness again. Jessica felt a shuffling around her, but was too dazed to move. She gasped as another match was lit, then breathed a sigh of relief when she saw the man holding it was Dylan. Carlton sat huddled on the floor two pews away.

"Jessica!" Dylan knelt beside her. "Are you all right?"

She nodded slowly. "Dylan, how...why..." She winced as she touched her fingers to her aching skull. "What are you doing here?"

"We'll talk about it later." He lit another match and gathered her close with one arm.

She couldn't stop the shiver running through her. "He was going to burn the church down, Dylan. All this time it was Carlton who wanted Stone Creek—for Myrna." She pushed away suddenly and tried to stand. "Hannibal! Carlton drugged him. He's by the back door."

Dylan helped her up, then made her sit on a pew. "I'll take care of him, but I'm going to get you back to the hotel first." He glanced over at Carlton, who rocked back and forth, his head in his hands.

"I can manage on my own. It's Carlton who needs help," she said quietly. Dylan started to protest, but she shook her head. "He's sick, Dylan. Please."

With a sigh, Dylan nodded. After he relit the altar candle, he helped Carlton to his feet. Jessica stood slowly, then

glanced around the church she'd come so close to losing.
She breathed a long sigh of relief and smiled.

"Thank you, Meggie and Lucas," she whispered softly.

"I still can't believe this."

Dylan watched Jake pace the floor in Jessica's bedroom.
The entire Stone family had arrived almost an hour ago and
congregated in the room, with Annie and Savannah sitting
on the bed where Dylan had insisted Jessica stay put. Emma
sat on the floor with Hannibal's head cradled in her lap. The
dog was still groggy, but opened his eyes and wagged his tail
every time Emma talked to him.

Jared sat on a chair in the corner, shaking his head.
"Carlton, of all people. Why would he risk everything to
buy a few acres of land for his daughter?"

"Stone Creek is hardly a few acres," Jake said.

"Myrna and Carlton don't know any other way to love
each other," Jessica said. "Money is all they have."

"You're right." Myrna stood at the bathroom door, her
eyes red and swollen from her tears. Carlton was lying down
on Dylan's bed, and she'd been in there with him since she'd
arrived.

Twisting her hands, the woman moved hesitantly into the
room. "Money has always been the basis for my relationship with my father. Bigger and better meant more love."
She squeezed her eyes shut. "The only problem was it was
never enough."

She started to cry then. Not the manipulating sniffles the
Stone children had seen over the years, but true heartfelt
tears. Savannah went to the woman and put her arms
around her.

"I'm so sorry," Myrna sobbed. "I didn't know. Please
believe me."

Jessica reached over and took Myrna's hand. "We called
the doctor, Myrna. Your father may have to go to the hospital."

She nodded. "He's ill. I didn't realize how ill. There's so much we haven't told each other."

"You can catch up," Jessica said gently.

"We haven't much time," Myrna whispered.

Jessica squeezed her stepmother's hand. "It'll be enough."

Dylan watched the exchange between Jessica and Myrna and he realized what true forgiveness was. Myrna's selfishness, and her father's obsession had nearly destroyed Jessica's dream. Yet here she was, comforting the woman.

He could learn a lot from her, he realized. About trust. About the truth.

He just didn't know if he was brave enough.

Jessica refused to stay in bed one minute longer.

She threw back the covers, pulled on her clothes and sneaked to the door. She was perfectly all right, for heaven's sake. A little bump on the head. It was certainly nothing for everybody to get so tied up in knots about. Besides, almost an entire day had passed. Even Dr. Sanders had said she was fine, that all she needed was a little bed rest. So she'd rested enough already.

Unfortunately Carlton hadn't been so lucky. He'd taken a turn for the worse after everything that had happened, and the doctor had admitted him into a hospital in Midland. Everyone, including Myrna, understood he wouldn't be coming home.

She peeked into the hallway, half expecting a guard outside her door. The coast was clear.

Quietly she tiptoed down the stairs, hesitating at every squeaky step. Savannah and Annie had fussed over her like mother hens all day, and Jared had nearly carried her back to bed when she'd tried to sneak out after dinner two hours ago.

She was fine, she'd tried to tell him. Perfectly all right.

Except that she was miserable.

But it had nothing to do with the bump on her head and everything to do with a certain six-foot-four dark-haired handsome foreman.

Dylan had left last night with barely a goodbye. He'd had the strangest look in his eyes when he stepped outside with Jared and Jake, and a few minutes later, she'd heard his bike roar out of town. The sound was like a knife through her heart.

She'd known he was leaving. She'd told herself that she was ready for it, that she could handle it. She'd even foolishly told him that she'd manage just fine after he left. Nothing could have been further from the truth.

There'd been a spark of hope last night when he'd shown up at the church. She'd thought for one insane moment that he'd come back for her. That maybe he'd realized—she paused at the foot of the stairs and closed her eyes—he loved her.

She ran her hand over the smooth oak banister and stared at the fine grain of wood. Dylan's hands had worked wonders with the wood. He had skillful hands, large and rough, gentle, yet demanding. The memory of those hands on her skin and the wonders he worked there brought a shiver to her.

She still didn't know why he'd come back last night. Perhaps she never would now.

She sighed, calling herself an idiot ten different ways for giving in to her pain. She'd move on with her life. Makeshift would keep her busy, keep her life full, even if her heart was empty.

Cautiously, expecting one of her wardens to jump out at her, Jessica moved into the kitchen.

It was empty. In fact, now that she thought about it, the hotel was quiet. Even Hannibal, who had recovered completely after sleeping most of the day, was nowhere to be seen. "Anybody here?"

No answer.

Hands on her hips, she glanced around the kitchen, then spied a note on the table.

Jess,
Thought you might like some privacy. Will stop by to check on you tomorrow.

The gang

P.S. We let Hannibal out. You might want to go look for him and maybe get some fresh air to clear your mind.

Jessica stared at the note in her hand. They'd left her! Without so much as a goodbye! One minute they were hovering, the next, poof! Gone.

She tapped her foot on the floor and folded her arms. They were up to something. She didn't know what, but she knew there was something funny going on.

Shaking her head, she grabbed the sweater on a hook by the back door and stepped outside. The air was cool and crisp, and a brilliant ceiling of stars sparkled overhead.

Hannibal was barking down the street by the church. Not an angry bark, more of an insistent, come-here-and-play-with-me bark. Shaking her head, she moved in the direction of the church, then went still as she noticed the light flickering through the leaded glass.

No! It wasn't possible.

It couldn't be happening again!

Her heart pounded as she crept toward the open front doors.

And when she looked inside, she froze.

Thirteen

There were candles everywhere. Dozens of them. Inside the doorway, along the pews, on the altar. They swayed to the soft music of Tchaikovsky like hundreds of tiny glowing ballerinas. She stared in amazement and wonder, mesmerized by the display of dancing flames.

And there were flowers. Baskets and vases overflowing with red roses and white lilies. Their sweet scent filled the church.

This was a dream. A beautiful dream. Breath held, she moved down the aisle, taking in every detail, afraid to blink and make everything disappear.

He stood at the end of the aisle, his expression intense, his eyes dark and sensual as he watched her. She stepped in front of him and spread her hands wide.

"Dylan," she whispered, "what is all this?"

"Tradition."

"Tradition?"

"I believe you told me that on special occasions, the people of Makeshift lit candles in the church."

Confused, she looked up at him. "I did, but—"

He put a finger to her lips. "I told you last night we would talk later. We never got that chance."

"You left," she said quietly, hoping her voice didn't sound as desperate as her heart felt.

"I couldn't stand it. Not being able to hold you, to crawl in that bed with you and pull your body against mine so I could hear your heartbeat and know you were safe."

She was sure he could hear her heartbeat now it was pounding so loud. "You could have."

He shook his head. "Your family had a big enough shock. I don't think Jared and Jake would take kindly to me climbing into your bed."

She lifted one corner of her mouth. "So you *are* afraid of my brothers," she teased.

He moved closer and gently took hold of her wrists, then placed her palms on his chest. "Do you feel that?"

His heart thundered in his chest. She nodded slowly, looking into his eyes.

"It's not your brothers I'm afraid of, Jessica, it's myself."

The movement of his fingers on her wrists created tiny electrical currents that coursed over her arms. It was all part of the dream, she decided, and gave herself up to it. Maybe that hit on the head was a good thing, after all.

"Dean came to see me," he went on. "Yesterday, right after you left Cactus Flat. He heard I was leaving, and he wanted me to take him and Troy with me."

Dean wanted to leave with Dylan? "But you can't—"

He pressed his thumb to her lips. "I know that. I told him no."

His thumb, which was now tracing her bottom lip, distracted her momentarily. She pulled in a slow breath, then reluctantly tugged his hand away. "How did he take it?"

"Not well. Oh, he pretended like it was fine, but I felt as if I'd thrown a puppy into the ocean."

Her heart went out to Dean. He'd known so much disappointment. "What did you do?"

"What I always do when I feel trapped—get the hell out. I started to pack my things when I picked up the gloves you gave me. I sat down and put them on, and thought how well they fit me, how perfect they are." He tilted up her chin and looked into her eyes. "Like you, Jessica."

She didn't dare to believe what he was saying. It frightened her. Because if she was wrong, if she misunderstood, she thought she might die.

"He told me to tell you I was sorry," Dylan said. "When I told him I had, he said, 'Maybe you should try harder.'" Dylan brought his face closer to hers. "That's what I'm doing, Jessica. I'm trying harder, as if my life depends on it. Because it does."

The hammering of her heart settled to a slow heavy thud. She leaned against him, certain her knees would give out if she didn't. "I—I don't know what to say."

"Say you love me." He brought his lips to hers, but his kiss was no more than a whisper.

The flames from the candles seemed to brighten; the smell of roses and lilies surrounded her. She felt his warm body against her own, felt his lips on hers. This wasn't a dream. It was real. "Dylan," she murmured, "the candles and roses. I don't need all this."

"*I* need it," he said gently. "I wanted to give you everything I've never given anyone before. Music and flowers, candlelight. And this..."

He pulled a small box out of his pocket and flipped it open. A cluster of tiny diamonds surrounded a single solitaire. The jewels sparkled in the candlelight.

All she could do was stare. She didn't even feel the beating of her heart anymore. She was numb. Eyes wide, she looked up at him. "You've certainly been busy today."

He frowned. "You're supposed to say, 'It's beautiful, Dylan. I love it.'"

She smiled back. "It's beautiful, Dylan," she whispered, and touched his cheek with her fingers. "I love you."

"And I love you."

He pulled her to him and kissed her like he never had before. It was a kiss that promised more, with nothing held back. A feeling of pure joy and exhilaration flowed through her.

"I don't know what I would've done if anything had happened to you last night," he said raggedly. "If you hadn't opened those doors in time, we might not be standing here."

She inched her face away from his. "I didn't open the doors."

"Of course you did. They were locked, then they flew open. That's what caused the wind that blew Carlton's match out."

"Dylan." She cupped his face in her hands. "I was on the floor. I'd already hit my head. And the wind was *not* from the doors opening."

He stared at her for a long time. "You can't mean..."

"Yes. I do."

He looked up and glanced around. "Meggie and Lucas?"

She nodded.

"Well, I'll be damned." His smile was one of amazement and acceptance. "I don't know how I'll ever thank them."

"You already have. You saved their church. That was Meggie crying last night when Carlton almost burned it down."

He stared into the shadows. "You think they're here right now?"

"Probably."

Still smiling, he looked down at her. "And do you think they approve?"

"Of what?"

"Me."

The flames brightened then and a small breeze drifted through, lifting the ends of their hair. Jessica laughed. "I'd say so."

He shook his head incredulously, then pulled her close again. "And what about your family?" he asked. "Do I have to go to Jared and Jake and ask for your hand?"

"You ask them for my hand and I'll give you the boot," she said indignantly. "I make my own decisions."

He lowered his head and brushed her lips with his. "You can make any decision you want after we're married. As long as it agrees with mine. Ouch!" He winced when she bit his lip.

There was a smile in her eyes as she looked at him. "Speaking of my family, they disappeared very mysteriously tonight. I don't suppose they had anything to do with all this, did they?"

He lifted his brows innocently. "Would we do anything behind your back, Jess?"

"I'm shocked you would even ask me that in a church."

His grin grew devilish. "If that shocks you, then wait till you hear this . . ."

He whispered in her ear what he wanted to do to her when they got back to the hotel. That night and the next and every night thereafter. She thrilled to his words. Breathless, she answered him, encouraged him, and when the last flame was gently extinguished, she led him back to the hotel and they let their own flame burn wild.

"Lucas, isn't it wonderful?" Meggie breathed in the scent of roses and nestled in the circle of Lucas's arms. *"They're going to be married. Right here, in our church."*

Lucas pulled her closer. "Yes, my love, almost as wonderful as the feel of you in my arms again."

She smiled softly at him. "I was so frightened last night when Carlton wanted to burn our church down. I am still amazed we were able to open those doors. Even for us, that was a difficult maneuver."

"It just goes to show how strong we are together," he said.

"And we will be together now, soon. Truly together, as we were meant to be." She touched his cheek. "Oh, Lucas, I've heard it's so beautiful there."

"You're beautiful," he whispered, and touched his lips to hers.

A cool breeze rustled the grass and spring-blooming bulbs the second Saturday in April. White puffy clouds scudded over the distant mountains, and the fresh scent of recent rain clung to the air.

A perfect day for a wedding.

Inside the church, garlands of baby's breath and pink roses draped the aisle, and huge bouquets of spring flowers covered the altar. The sound of Beethoven's Ninth filled the church from the new organ, one of many donations that had poured in since the review board had approved Makeshift Youth Center as a certified camp and counseling center.

The pews were crowded with anxious family and friends, among them Dean and Troy in their Sunday best. Their father sat beside them. Thanks to Dylan's persistence, three months in a twelve-step program for father and sons had brought them all close together again.

Myrna sat in the front row where Jessica had insisted she sit, though the woman had argued she didn't deserve the honor. With Carlton gone, Myrna was putting her time and money into working with needy children. Amazingly, when Makeshift Youth Center opened in two weeks, Myrna would be head administrator and chief benefactor.

When the organ boomed out the first thundering chords of Handel's "Wedding March," everyone straightened, then stood as the bride slowly glided down the aisle.

Jessica held on tightly to her bouquet and moved forward on knees that felt like water. Jake walked beside her, his hand on her arm giving reassurance and encouragement. She glanced sideways at him and he winked at her. She smiled, then focused her attention on the man waiting by the altar.

He wore a tux well, she thought with pride. The juxtaposition of suave against rugged, debonair against masculine, was devastating. His heated gaze followed her as she moved closer. *Slow deep breaths,* she remembered Annie and Savannah advising her, and gripped the lace handkerchief that had been her great-great-grandmother's.

"You okay?" Jake whispered.

She nodded. "Okay" would hardly describe what she was. The love she felt for Dylan swelled inside her, and though she'd promised herself she wouldn't, she felt tears burn her eyes. A few feet more... a few minutes more...

He couldn't take his eyes off her. His throat had gone dry when she'd stepped into the church. She was a vision in antique white lace. His black bow tie and cummerbund felt tight. His palms were damp. Jared stood behind him, as did Savannah, Annie and Emma.

Family. He was going to be part of a family. He still couldn't believe it, no more than he could believe it possible to love one woman more than life itself.

Their eyes locked as she moved in front of him. He reached out to her, and as Jake stepped away, he took her hand in his and led her to the altar.

Together, hand in hand, they turned.

The minister smiled and opened his book.

The ceremony was brief, as both Dylan and Jessica had requested, and as they said their vows, a cool breeze swept gently through the church.

"I, Jessica, take Dylan Grant..."

"I, Meggie, take Lucas..."

"I, Dylan, take Jessica Stone..."

"I, Lucas, take Meggie..."

Dylan pulled Jessica into his arms and sealed their vows with a kiss and a whispered "I love you." Smiling, Jessica repeated his words.

And as they turned to be congratulated as Mr. and Mrs. Dylan Grant, the fading outline of another bride and groom disappeared.

Eyes wide, Dylan looked at her, and she at him. They smiled slowly, and as Dylan circled her waist with one arm and hurried her down the aisle, she said a silent goodbye, knowing that her life, her heart and her legacy of Stone Creek would never die.

* * * * *

SILHOUETTE® Desire®

COMING NEXT MONTH

#973 WOLFE WEDDING—Joan Hohl
Big Bad Wolfe
No one ever thought January's *Man of the Month*, Cameron Wolfe, was the marrying kind. But a romantic getaway with brainy beauty Sandra Bradley suddenly had the lone wolf thinking about a Wolfe wedding!

#974 MY HOUSE OR YOURS?—Lass Small
The last thing Josephine Morris wanted was to let her infuriating ex, Chad Wilkins, permanently back into her life. Yet when he proposed they have a wild, romantic *affair,* Jo just couldn't say no....

#975 LUCAS: THE LONER—Cindy Gerard
Sons and Lovers
Lucas Caldwell knew better than to trust the sultry reporter who suddenly appeared on his ranch. But Kelsey Gates wouldn't stop until she got her story—or her man!

#976 PEACHY'S PROPOSAL—Carole Buck
Wedding Belles
Peachy Keene just wasn't going to live her life as a virgin! So she proposed a no-strings affair with dashing Luke Devereaux—and got much more than she bargained for.

#977 COWBOY'S BRIDE—Barbara McMahon
Single dad Trace Longford would do anything to make new neighbor Kalli Bonotelli sell her ranch to him. But now the rugged cowboy not only wanted her ranch—he wanted Kalli, too!

#978 SURRENDER—Metsy Hingle
Aimee Lawrence had found Mr. Right—but he insisted she sign a prenuptial agreement! Now he had to prove his feelings for her ran much deeper than lust—or there would be *no* wedding....

MILLION DOLLAR SWEEPSTAKES (III)

Silhouette

SPECIAL EDITION™

CELEBRATION 1000

It's our 1000th Special Edition and we're celebrating!

Join us these coming months for some wonderful stories in a special celebration of our 1000th book with some of your favorite authors!

Diana Palmer
Debbie Macomber
Phyllis Halldorson

Nora Roberts
Christine Flynn
Lisa Jackson

Plus miniseries by:

Lindsay McKenna, Marie Ferrarella, Sherryl Woods and Gina Ferris Wilkins.

And many more books by special writers!

And as a special bonus, all Silhouette Special Edition titles published during Celebration 1000! will have _**double**_ Pages & Privileges proofs of purchase!

Silhouette Special Edition...heartwarming stories packed with emotion, just for you! You'll fall in love with our next 1000 special stories!

1000BK-R

THE PROTECTORS

Trained to protect, ready to lay their lives on the line, but unprepared for the power of love.

Award-winning author Beverly Barton brings you Ashe McLaughlin, Sam Dundee and J. T. Blackwood... three rugged, sexy ex-government agents—each with a special woman to protect.

Embittered former DEA Agent Sam Dundee has a chance at romance in GUARDING JEANNIE, IM #688, coming in January 1996. Hired to protect Jeannie Alverson, the woman who saved his life years ago, Sam is faced with his greatest challenge ever...guarding his heart and soul from her loving, healing hands.

And coming in April 1996, the trilogy's exciting conclusion. Look for J. T. Blackwood's story, BLACKWOOD'S WOMAN, IM #707.

To order your copy of the first book in THE PROTECTORS series, Ashe McLaughlin's story, DEFENDING HIS OWN (IM #670), please send your name, address, zip or postal code along with a check or money order (please do not send cash) for $3.75 ($4.25 in Canada) plus 75¢ postage and handling ($1.00 in Canada), payable to Silhouette Books, to:

In the U.S.	In Canada
Silhouette Books	Silhouette Books
3010 Walden Ave.	P. O. Box 636
P. O. Box 9077	Fort Erie, Ontario
Buffalo, NY 14269-9077	L2A 5X3

Please specify book title(s) with your order.
Canadian residents add applicable federal and provincial taxes.   BBPROT2

You're About to Become a
Privileged Woman

Reap the rewards of fabulous free gifts and benefits with proofs-of-purchase from Silhouette and Harlequin books

Pages & Privileges™

It's our way of thanking you for buying our books at your favorite retail stores.

PROOF OF PURCHASE

SD-PP83

Offer expires October 31, 1996

Harlequin and Silhouette—
the most privileged readers in the world!

For more information about Harlequin and Silhouette's PAGES & PRIVILEGES program call the Pages & Privileges Benefits Desk: 1-503-794-2499

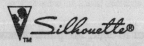